The Outlaw Life

When Chase Carver dragged himself into Mammoth Springs he was cold, hungry and exhausted and any man in that condition will gratefully accept the help of a stranger. But the stranger led him to an outlaw stronghold, filled with cutthroats, thieves and gunmen. After joining the outlaws on a bank job, and earning himself the name 'Mad Dog' Carver, both the county sheriff and the army are now hot on his tail.

And by rescuing two young women from the ruthless Bandolero he has committed a crime against criminals and faces the entire outlaw contingent who are ready to take up arms against him. The outlaw life had been easy to fall into but there is going to be a fight to the death to try and crawl back out of it. . . .

The Outlaw Life

Owen G. Irons

A Black Horse Western

ROBERT HALE · LONDON

ISBN 978-0-7090-9569-9

Robert Hale Limited
Clerkenwell House
Clerkenwell Green
London EC1R 0HT

www.halebooks.com

Typeset by
Derek Doyle & Associates, Shaw Heath
Printed and bound in Great Britain by
CPI Antony Rowe, Chippenham and Eastbourne

ONE

Chase Carver could smell the cold. He had never thought of it before. He knew that you could smell the heat that rose from the desert floor at midday, but he had never smelled cold before. It smelled like marble slabs, iron beams, clotting blood, and vaguely like death. Just then, he was too cold to ponder this curious idea. He was too cold to move, to think.

He had ridden down out of the high country, moving quickly after some encouragement. His horse had broken its leg on a rocky mountain slope, and Chase had walked the rest of the way – two days' travel – to Mammoth Springs where he now sat, blanket pulled over his shoulders, draped over his knees.

Without a dollar in his pocket he had tried to find a nest in the hayloft of a stable, but had been rousted out of there with a warning. His next thought was to try to find a restaurant, any place where the heat from the stove might lend a touch of warmth to an outside wall. There he had settled – sitting against the outside wall of a restaurant kitchen, but now as midnight approached, the stove had been allowed to go out, the wall began to cool. It was a frozen, hellish night he faced.

There was a grove of live oak trees across the alley. Their shadows in the starlight were bright objects in the deep blackness of night. Chase shifted slightly. Only a little; he could not lose the meager warmth he had collected, huddled inside his blanket. His bones seemed frozen, as brittle as ice; his muscles were a collection of cold, aching knots.

When the back door of the restaurant opened, allowing a brief wafting of warmer air from inside, his eyes scuttled hopefully in that direction. But the door was pulled shut as suddenly as it had been opened. The shadow from within had thrown some scraps out into the alley – a handful of biscuits and what seemed to be, smelled like, beef ribs.

Chase, who had not eaten for two days, was grateful for the food if not for the manner of serving. He flung his blanket aside and scrabbled toward the bits of kitchen refuse. A fierce throaty growl met his ears.

Chase found himself face to face with a pair of crouching yellow curs who must have been the intended recipients of the restaurant waste. They obviously took it as their due as they slunk forward, hackles rising, bared fangs white in the night. Desperation caused Chase to grab one of the rib bones nearly from the jaws of one of the mongrel dogs and roll away. His hand was on his holstered Colt revolver, and he realized that he was in desperate enough condition to consider shooting two scrounging dogs to take their food.

He leaned back against the wall again, and tore at the meat remaining on the rib with his teeth, watching the dogs of night gobble the biscuits, taking them down with one swallow apiece, then circle threateningly around him, snapping, as they snatched up the rib bones one by one. Their eyes were feral, their jaws slavered. They were beasts on the fringe of existence, sustained only by the cook who tossed them their meager rations each night then quickly closed the door.

Chase was no better. He pawed at the bone, his pistol held on his lap until the wild dogs had finished. Then they scuttled away into the darkness, and for a brief angry moment Chase found himself envying these wild things. They at least had a hidden den somewhere where they could curl up together and use each other's body heat to survive one more bitterly cold night.

He closed his eyes and tried to sleep, but it was a futile attempt. Sleep would not come as his toes seemed to freeze in his boots, as his teeth chattered and his shoulders shivered uncontrollably. He hadn't heard the man approach him, but his voice was clear, near at hand.

'Well, aren't you a sight to see! Sleeping out in an alley, scrapping with dogs for their food. Aren't you a miserable sight?'

Chase supposed he was, but he felt offended that someone had pointed it out to him, that someone had witnessed his degradation. He looked up at the tall, indistinct shadow of the man standing over him. Angular and narrow, wearing a sheepskin-lined coat – that was all that Chase could make out in the darkness.

'I didn't know what else to do,' Chase said. 'I haven't got any money. I don't know anyone in this town.'

'What's that got to do with anything!' the man laughed. 'You got a gun, I see.'

'I don't understand you.'

'You better start learning,' the shadowy stranger said. 'Unless you want to end your days like this. Come on. Get up! I can see you need some education.'

With some effort Chase unwound his cold, cramped muscles and rose to his feet. He was half a head taller than his new companion, who wore a short shaggy beard and a low-slung revolver on his bony hip. With Chase hobbling along beside him, the stranger led the way to the head of the alley, pausing to retrieve his bay horse which had been tied to a scrub oak tree. As his circulation returned to something near normal, Chase began to feel better although he had no idea where they were heading.

The main street of town was alight with lanterns which seemed to glow in every window. The saloons they passed were active, raucously so. Warm air drifted from the doors which were constantly opening and closing as men of all descriptions went in and out, frequently to welcoming shouts. Chase, who was a man of the mountains, had never seen such a sight – mock hilarity, cursing and fighting in the streets.

'Where are we going?' he asked his companion. 'And who are you?'

'The name's Tucker, Jeb Tucker,' the bearded man said without glancing back. 'And we are going to find you a hot meal and a bed.'

'I haven't got any money,' Chase said. 'Not a nickel.'

'I don't remember asking you if you did,' Tucker answered. 'Ah, there it is – the Trails' End Hotel, and a fine-looking establishment it is.' He indicated with his chin a two-story wooden building with gingerbread along the eaves.

'Are you staying there?' Chase asked.

'I will be,' Tucker replied, 'and so will you.'

'But. . . .' Chase said as he watched Tucker tie his bay horse to the hitch rail in front of the hotel.

'You just be quiet, boy. I do the talking. Get me?'

'Yes,' Chase said meekly. Together they tramped up the steps and entered the hotel. On plush settees positioned around the rear wall of the hotel, ladies in feathered hats, wearing silk dresses, sat speaking in soft tones to well-dressed, well-groomed men in town suits. These paused in their conversation to look at the two rough-dressed men as they entered.

Tucker strode directly toward the counter, striding across the hotel lobby as if he owned the place. Chase followed, his eyes cast down. He was grateful for the warmth around him. His shivering had finally stopped and his muscles worked free and easy again.

There was a balding man wearing gold pince-nez glasses and sporting a wide scarlet tie of a type Chase had never seen before, leaning forward behind the counter, watching their approach without pleasure.

'I'll take a room with two beds,' Tucker said in a gravelly voice.

'Very well, sir,' the clerk said with manufactured politeness, reaching for the hotel register. It is customary to pay in advance,' he said, looking the two up and down. He continued to hold the pen in his hand, not offering it to Tucker.

'Why, you scoundrel,' Tucker said loudly enough to be heard across the lobby. 'I ain't paying for something I haven't got yet. Do you pay for your meal before you've eaten?'

'Sir,' the clerk said with stiff, forced politeness, 'it is the policy of this establishment—'

'You are starting to offend me,' Tucker said, folding his arms on the counter top. 'What is it? Do you think we are a couple of drag-arounds who can't afford a night's rest in your beautiful hotel? Look at this,' he said, straightening. Tucker had thrust his hand deep into the pocket of his twill trousers and pulled out a handful of coins. From where he stood, Chase could see the glitter of twenty-dollar gold pieces.

'I will pay you in the morning if everything is satisfactory,' Tucker said. His voice had dropped to a low rumble. 'I am not accustomed to being treated this way.' Again his voice, loud in the room, caused heads to turn.

The clerk glanced at the hotel's other patrons, looked at a younger man in a blue suit who was standing at his shoulder, then turned the register and handed Tucker the pen. Tucker scrawled his name on the broad page of the register. The clerk took a key from a hook on a wall board behind him, glanced at it, at Tucker, at the younger man and slid it across the counter to Tucker.

'Thanks,' Tucker said sourly. 'You've got a kitchen, don't you? Send us up two steaks, two baked potatoes and a mess of pinto beans.' He turned sharply toward Chase. 'Come on, kid! A hell of a way they have of doing business, isn't it?' He tramped away toward the staircase leading to the second floor, Chase in his wake, the other guests staring after them.

The room was larger than Chase had expected, blessedly warm. Two single beds stood against opposite walls. There were thick blue-flowered coverlets on the beds. A washbasin stood in one corner, a dresser supporting a mirror in another. A thick rust-red carpet covered the floor. It was the fanciest room Chase Carver had seen in his short life.

Jeb Tucker had already tugged off his boots and

removed his sheepskin. His gun remained belted on his hips. Chase sat on his own bed and watched the man wonderingly. Chase could think of nothing he had done to deserve such kindness. After about half an hour two young men in white shirts came in, placing a narrow wooden table between them. There were two platters containing steak, baked potatoes and pinto beans as Tucker had requested.

'Boys,' Tucker said, 'I'll be leaving a handsome tip for you when I check out. One other thing – I left my horse out front.' He described the bay as he seated himself at the low table and tucked a napkin behind his collar. 'I'd appreciate it if one of you would take it to the stable for me. If you can't go, find a kid who would like to earn a few bucks.'

With everyone thanking each other all around, the two smiling employees backed out of the room, bowing.

'Pull that chair up to the table, Chase,' Tucker said. 'Or do you demand the encouragement of dogs?'

Chase required no encouragement; he had just been waiting for the invitation. He set to work on the steak with a sharp hotel knife, and forked potato into his mouth. He forced himself to eat slowly, knowing the surprise his deprived stomach was receiving. Nothing could have been better. There was not a thing left on their plates when they had finished eating save for a few scraps of fat. Chase yawned and felt his body swoon; he could not stay awake much longer.

Beneath the coverlet and two blankets, his head resting on a down pillow, Chase felt himself sinking into a warm, comfortable, longed-for sleep. He muttered in Tucker's direction:

'There's no way I can thank you enough for—'

'Shut up and get your rest. Sometime, some way, we'll find a way for you to pay me back.'

Chase tried to answer, to nod, but his full belly and the warmth of the bed allowed only an inarticulate gurgle to pass his lips. Sleep was bliss. The world was good once more.

The morning sun was a red blur against the hotel window which was frosted by the night's chill. Chase had no wish to rise from his bed ever again. Tugging the blankets up over his shoulders, he smiled. The world had grown warmer, kinder, and he owed it all to this man, Tucker, whom he barely knew. He would always feel gratitude toward that whiskered, narrow man.

Rolling his head, he could see that Tucker was already half-risen from his bed. He sat with his blanket over his hunched shoulders, his eyes red with the night's sleep, trembling just a little with the new morning's nip. Tucker noticed the stirring in Chase's bed and flicked his gaze that way.

'Roll out, kid. I like to be moving early.'

Chase nodded, reaching for his boots. Both men dressed in silence. The window lightened as the sun faded from red to yellow. Beyond the glass a stand of cottonwood trees quaked in the breeze which had arrived with the dawn.

13

'Where are we going?' Chase asked when he had finished dressing, adding his gunbelt to his costume.

'To get you a horse,' Tucker said roughly. Both men seemed to assume that they were to be traveling together now. To Chase, a babe in this new environment, it was comforting to know the wily old man would be playing the role of mentor.

Stepping out into the corridor of the hotel, they found themselves alone. There were no other early-risers. The others who had paid for their beds meant to make the best possible use of them, it seemed.

They walked down the staircase to the empty lobby. Behind the counter stood a different hotel clerk than the one they had met the night before. Tucker raised his hand in the clerk's direction, nodded, and continued on toward the outside door. The clerk gave them only a casual glance. Chase waited until they were outside before he asked Tucker:

'Didn't you owe them some money?'

'I took care of that last night,' Tucker answered. 'Now where's that stable?'

'I saw two of them off this way – to the right,' Chase said. 'I suppose the hotel would use the nearest one, don't you?'

'I s'pose,' Tucker replied. His manner seemed a little colder this morning. Hands thrust deep into his pockets, Chase followed Tucker down the rime-encrusted muddy street toward the nearest stable.

Inside they found the night-man, his own eyes encrusted with sleep, his teeth chattering. He was red-headed, buck-toothed, and very tall. Tucker walked up to this scarecrow of a man and said:

'Come to pick up my bay – there he is over there.'

'Sure. Two dollars will do it,' the scarecrow said with a toothy smile.

'What!' Tucker's face grew red. He tilted his face toward the stableman's. 'Look here, friend, I sent one of the hotel boys over here last night with coin to pay for my pony's feed and board. Someone's trying to gyp me – I'm not paying twice for the same service!'

'I didn't know. . . .' the stableman stuttered in the face of Tucker's rage. 'M-mostly men pay when they come to pick up their horses. I . . . I didn't,' he stammered uncertainly. 'Maybe the hotel boy didn't. . . .'

'Maybe he didn't,' Tucker said more calmly. 'Or maybe someone in this stable took the money and neglected to tell you – I won't stand for it either way.' His hand rested on the butt of his holstered Colt revolver as he spoke, his jaw jutting forward. The stablehand who was unarmed and seemed to be of an uncombative nature watched stiffly, his Adam's apple quivering. Tucker's aspect changed.

'Look, son,' he said more gently, 'if there's been a mistake, I'll see that it's made up to you.' His hand had dipped into his pocket and he displayed the gold double-eagles that Chase had seen in the hotel. 'My friend here needs a horse and tack. I'll be happy to give you a few dollars more than you're asking for a good set-up.' Without turning his head, Tucker told Chase, 'Find a pony you like, son.'

Chase wandered the stable aisle while Jeb Tucker and the stableman dickered over a tooled saddle. There was a neat little blue roan, four or five years old, with slender legs standing watching his approach. It was more lightly built than Chase's own mountain horse, but he was no longer in the mountains where muscle was all and speed came second.

'Is this blue roan for sale?' Chase called.

'It is now,' the stablehand called back in a voice that cracked. 'Man brought it in a week ago and left it – we don't hold 'em any longer than that without someone brings us some payment.'

'Bring it out, son,' Tucker said, and Chase fixed a bridle to the pony and led it toward Tucker.

Running a hand over the roan's flank, Tucker said, 'Looks neat to me. Take it for a ride.'

'Wait a minute,' the stablehand objected. 'We can't be turning a horse free like that!'

'The kid just wants to ride it to the end of town and back. Would you buy a horse you never rode? Besides, I'm standing here with money in my pocket, am I not? Go ahead, kid – take this saddle.'

The stablehand watched dubiously as Chase saddled the blue roan, but with a smiling Tucker leaning against a stall partition, his pockets full of gold money, the man shrugged off his doubts.

'See if it's got any speed,' Tucker said to Chase as he swung into leather. 'End of the street and back, all right? Then we can haggle with our friend here.'

Cocking his head, Chase nodded and walked the spry little horse out of the stable. It was still early in the morning; the streets were nearly empty and the pony seemed ready to run, and so Chase nudged the horse with his heels and let it out, running at a brisk pace toward the end of town.

The animal was willing, young, and strong. Chase pulled up in an oak grove at the outskirts of town, and patted the blue roan's neck, listening to it breathe a minute before racing back. He never had the opportunity. Before he could start back along his intended course, he spotted Tucker astride his bay horse riding toward him. Reaching him, Tucker asked:

'How is he?'

'Quick. Sound as a bell,' Chase said with a smile.

'Good. Then let's get riding. We have some miles to cover.'

Tucker started on before Chase could ask him a question. Drawing alongside, he asked it:

'What about the stable? They'll want to be paid for the horse.'

'I took care of that,' Tucker said without glancing his way, without slowing his bay, and they made their way out on to the long plains, riding who-knew where.

TWO

It was a long morning under a heated sun. Chase studied the panorama around him. He had never been this far south. Most of his life had been spent in the high places – the Sangre de Cristo mountains where Moss Wheaton had his sprawling Timberline, Colorado ranch. The land here was mostly rolling to flat, of red earth with virtually no greenery except for patches of sage and scattered greasewood. It was unusual to the eye and not entirely soothing to the spirit. Farther south he could see the low, dark spine of a mountain range, which Tucker told him were the Guadalupes, stretching from New Mexico Territory into Texas. From his point of view the mountains seemed mostly barren and unforested, a far different type of land than the snow-capped, pine-deep Rocky Mountains he was accustomed to. He followed on doggedly, trusting Tucker to know the way – to wherever they were headed.

In the early afternoon they halted at a narrow-running reddish creek and dismounted to rest and water the horses and to eat. The bluffs lining the stream were lined with willows. The high sun glittered off the slowly running water. The dust they had dragged in with them continued to hang in the air for a long time. Tucker immediately got to work building a small fire with dried willow brush. He had a black iron flying pan near at hand, ready to cook with.

'You'll find a wax-paper bundle in my saddle-bags, Chase. Fetch it for me, will you?' Chase found the described bundle and took it to Tucker, who was crouched over a low-burning, nearly smokeless fire.

'Well, open it up!' Tucker said sharply and Chase unwrapped the package to find two thick, pink rib-eye steaks. He raised his eyebrows in surprise.

'Where did. . . ?'

'I got those from the hotel kitchen last night while you were sleeping. We had to have some provisions.'

'Steak for a noon meal!' Chase was astonished.

'You have to eat. Might as well eat well,' Tucker answered, throwing a steak into the pan to sizzle.

Tucker was a puzzle, Chase was thinking as he washed out the pan and their tin plates at the streamside after eating, using sand to scour the frying pan. How had he fallen in with him? Well, simple necessity on his part had caused that, but what did Tucker want with him? He was an added expense to the narrow man. Already he had cost him a hotel lodging, supper at the hotel, and the price of the blue roan and a fancy saddle, which could not have come cheaply. Chase was grateful, but he had not yet come to believe in charitable angels descending to his aid. Chase determined to ask Tucker his questions if he could find a way of doing it without insulting his generosity.

The sun was wheeling slowly toward the west as they started on again, but there were hours of daylight still ahead. The desert land had become warm and now grew hot as they continued on their way. The sky was totally free of clouds – they would have another cold night to follow the hot day.

A red dust devil which seemed to have pursued them along their way spun off and dissipated before the fitful wind. The earth underfoot began to grow stony. Black volcanic rocks lay scattered around them. Chase's mouth was dry. It seemed not to be the time for talking. It was Tucker who broke the long silence, riding his horse up beside the little blue roan.

'Where'd you say you came from?' Tucker asked.

'Over in Colorado. I got myself thrown off the home spread, got my horse's leg broken. I walked the rest of the way to Mammoth Springs – two days without food and only what little water I could find in calderas and such.'

'Thrown off, huh,' Tucker said thoughtfully, keeping his whiskered face fixed on the trail ahead.

'Well, you see,' Chase said, 'I was working for a man named Moss Wheaton up near a town called Timberline. He had a daughter named Laura. Laura Wheaton is the prettiest girl you'll ever see.

Her hair—'

'I can do without all of that,' Tucker said. 'I never met a man who hasn't been in love with the prettiest girl in the world – and one who didn't make an effort to ruin his life for him.'

Chase, who had temporarily been lost in reverie, was offended by the rebuke – not for his sake, but for Laura's. Nevertheless, if Tucker didn't like the conversation, he would veer away from it.

After another few minutes Tucker looked curiously at him and asked, 'Were you. . . ?'

'No,' Chase said hastily, anticipating the rest of the question. 'Wheaton just didn't want his daughter wasting her time on a drifting cowboy. One with no money.'

'I got you,' Tucker said. 'The story never changes no matter how many times I hear it. A man without money hasn't got a chance in this world. Oh, a girl will tell you it doesn't matter to her, but wait until she has to live without it! You just rode out, then?'

'With a few bullets chasing me,' Chase said, smiling narrowly at the memory. 'I don't think anyone was trying to hit me, but I got the message.'

Now, he supposed, was the time to ask the question he had on his mind. 'Tucker? Why is it you helped me out?'

'You were there. You saw what you had become – fighting with those curs over a few scraps of garbage. I won't see any man reduced to living like a dog.'

'Is that all there was to it?' Chase asked as

21

Tucker's eyes drifted away again.

'Mostly,' the older man said. It was obvious he was through talking. Chase did ask, 'Mind telling me where we're riding?'

'Bandolero,' Tucker muttered.

'What's that?' Chase asked. 'I mean, I know what a *bandolero* is, but is this place you're talking about a town, a ranch, or. . . ?'

'It's a place for men like us,' Tucker said as if he were chewing carefully on the words before he let them escape his mouth.

Tucker was providing no more information now. Both men fell silent as they rode on across the New Mexico desert toward the Texas land ahead.

They camped an hour before sunset beside a creek which had no name, or if it had, Tucker failed to mention it. The sun reddened as it lowered itself toward the Guadalupes, which were distant and dim, flanked with shadows. The little stream itself blushed red and shone with brilliant copper veins. A pair of dragonflies droned past just above the water's surface, and distantly, a lonesome coyote howled a complaint to the darkening skies.

Tucker had started a small fire in a circle of rocks as Chase was seeing to the horses. Walking back, Chase could smell sausage frying and he thought again how lucky he was that Tucker had adopted him for the trail.

'You sure plan ahead, don't you?' Chase said as he crouched beside Tucker by the low-flickering fire. 'Sausage!'

22

'I persuaded the hotel cook to let me have 'em. As for planning ahead, I try to, kid, but when does it ever really do a man much good? I think of all the plans I have made in my life, and I. . . .' His words broke off and he shook his head heavily.

Later, relatively well fed, both men lay on their backs on the sandy shore of the little creek and watched as the silver stars awoke across the sky. An owl hooted from somewhere in the willows, but other than that there was only the constant, whispering sound of the flowing stream. Tucker had a small pipe filled with black tobacco and now he lit it with a twig from the dying camp-fire. His smoke rose into the air as he lay back, hands behind his head. He was inclined toward conversation on this night.

'It's an easy life, Chase. Easy if a man doesn't get too greedy,' he said out of the darkness. 'It's the greed, the need to make a big spectacle of himself that brings a man down. Mostly gets him killed for his troubles.

'What we have is a world where a man with a gun and a little nerve can get by very well without risking jail time or his life.'

Chase was making connections in his mind. He rolled on his side to face Tucker. 'Like hotel rooms, horses and such?' he asked. He both admired Tucker's nerve and despised himself for being a part of it. Except, he could remember too well how it felt to be afoot, starving, and cold to the bone.

'That's the kind of thief I am,' Tucker mused, holding his pipe where he could study the curlicue of tobacco smoke it raised. 'I take what I need and little more. I don't give anyone a reason to want to stretch my neck, to lock me away. If I'm cornered I can usually buy my way out with the little cash money I always carry. It's not like they make me swallow the dagger when I'm caught.'

Chase frowned in bewilderment. 'I don't get you, Tucker. "Swallow the dagger". What's that mean? I've never heard it before.'

'No, I don't guess you would have. It's not a thing you actually do, understand – though I did once see a man in a Kansas City circus do just that. What I'm talking about is on the outlaw trail you can't expect things to go as you like. All of the fame and fortune ahead of you can prove to be just . . .' he glanced at the pipe he held, 'a pipe dream.

'One day the sheriff comes,' Tucker continued, leaning forward now, his knees drawn up. 'Or a posse from an angry town. It could be a rival gang someone has crossed. Well, Chase, they find a man backed up in a canyon or in some town with his back against the wall, or approach him with a noose, there ain't no way out. He just has to swallow the dagger.'

'You mean pay the price for what he's done?'

'If you want to put it that way. Most of these fellows bring it on themselves. They feel like they got to have something they don't have. Need to have it. Well, me, I figure I've gotten along without it before and I'm not going to swallow the dagger over a new horse, a shipment of gold ... or a woman. All of which I've seen happen.'

'But still, the way you go about things, Tucker,' Chase said seriously as the fire burned low and the coyote sang again in the distance. 'It's sort of a dangerous way to live, isn't it?'

'Any way a man lives is dangerous,' Tucker said, leaning back, tilting his hat over his eyes as night settled. 'Ever think about a man who works in a coal mine every day? I have! Men who live like that are crazy if you ask me. A gun and a little nerve – that's all it takes for an easy life. So long as a man keeps this side of the dagger.'

He cocked himself up on one elbow and said, 'Do you think a man with a badge is going to come from Mammoth Springs because someone skipped on a hotel bill? That would be a laugh – something that probably happens every day.'

'Stealing a horse is a hanging offense,' Chase said doubtfully. He glanced toward the river's edge where the blue roan was picketed.

'You see!' Tucker said to himself, lying back again. 'You don't pay attention, boy! It's no wonder I found you eating with dogs.' There was some sarcasm in Tucker's voice, but Chase let it slide off him. 'Whose horse was that?' Tucker asked Chase.

'The stablehand said someone had left it there, couldn't pay his bill.'

'That's right. It didn't belong to the stable, nor to

that man. Its owner had abandoned it. All that stable-hand was interested in was making sure I had paid for the bay's feed and lodging. I could have continued to lay that off on the hotel boys, but I didn't. After you were gone I slipped him a ten-dollar gold piece and told him, "You never seen us after I picked up my horse." '

'For all his boss knows, the man who left the roan snuck away with it. For all the boss can tell, he hasn't lost much but a horse he would have to feed for free. For all the boss cares, he at least got the pay for my bay's care. For all the stablehand cares, he found himself in good with his boss and had a few dollars extra in his poke.

'Think anyone's going to run to the law over that?'

'I guess not,' Chase muttered into his blanket as he drew it up more tightly against the chill of the desert night. For all of the qualms he felt about Tucker's way of making his way through this world, he still harbored a grudging admiration for this des-perado who knew how to work his schemes without great risk to himself and little harm to any of his 'victims'.

And there was Chase's gratitude toward Tucker. He hadn't liked it when Tucker mentioned the night with the dogs again, but it was the truth and Tucker was the man who had taken one mongrel along with him, fed him, and given him a warm place to sleep. Perhaps he would continue to ride with Tucker for just a little while, learn a few new tricks.

Jeb Tucker was not a greedy nor violent man. He was just a cagey customer who knew how to live well without making or spending much money. It seemed an easy way to travel, with little to fear in the way of retribution. Hardly the same as these bank robbers and hold-up artists one heard about who inevitably were last seen on a gallows or swinging beneath a tree by their necks.

So long as a man avoided getting himself in a situation where he might have to 'swallow the dagger', the outlaw life seemed to have points to recommend it.

Tucker was the first to rise in the morning. Chase could see the older man standing against the red dawn sky in silhouette, his thumbs hooked in his gunbelt. Hearing Chase stir in his bed, the outlaw turned his head toward him.

'Nothing for breakfast this morning, kid,' Tucker said, 'but it doesn't matter much. In a few hours we'll be in Bandolero. There's grub there. Saddle your pony and let's ride before the sun heats up.'

They started on. The shadows beneath the yucca and clumps of nopal cactus, of which there were plenty, shortened and then vanished beneath the plants as the sun rode high and beat down unmercifully. The little blue roan now began to grow irritable as the day wore on.

'How much farther?' Chase asked through parched lips as they halted at a rocky ledge overlooking a twisted red ravine.

27

'Not that far,' Tucker said with some annoyance. 'I expected to find water down below, but I don't see a sign of it. It must've been a dry winter.'

By chance or design, Tucker did find a small trickle of water farther along where a thick stand of willows and cattails crowded up against the edge of a brackish pool. Bothersome armies of mosquitoes and gnats haunted the scum-coated pond. Chase used a dry stick to clear a drinking hole for his horse.

It was deathly hot. Chase seated himself in the scant shade of the willows to sit cross-legged beside Tucker, and watched his horse. 'I hope that water is good,' he said, not liking the prospect they faced if bad water poisoned their ponies.

Tucker, who had brought his canteen with him, passed it to Chase and said, 'It is. That bay of mine can smell arsenic, alkali or anything else that might be in it. He wouldn't so much as dip his muzzle in if there was anything wrong with the water.'

Chase drank tepid water from his canteen, wiped the sweat from his eyes and briefly watched as a red-tailed hawk screamed out something from the bright sky and dove earthward. Then it was silent. Only the cattails ruffling in the desert breeze, the hum of the swarms of mosquitoes and gnats around them.

'Chase,' Tucker said, looking up with those pouched eyes of his, 'can I ask you this: what do you think of me?'

The unexpected question briefly stumped Chase.

What was he to say? What sort of response did Tucker expect? He answered carefully.

'I think you're a man who knows his way around. I know you to be generous – look what you've done for me. Maybe you're a little bit secretive, but what man in your line of work wouldn't be?'

Tucker nodded, mulling the words. He suddenly said, quite loudly, 'I'm small fry!' His voice was loud enough to startle the horses. The blue roan stamped a hind foot. 'I'm more rat than fox,' he went on more quietly.

'Now, Tucker. . . .' Chase interrupted.

'Let me finish first, kid,' Tucker said, holding up a hand. 'There's a reason I've said that. It's a warning in part. I've got no reputation in Bandolero – as you'll find when we get there. I'm about the lowest-rated man in the camp there. I'm tolerated, nothing more.'

'I'm sure. . . .' Chase began, embarrassed by Tucker's admission. The older man cut him off again.

'It's the truth, you'll see that. Bandolero is home to some of the toughest, meanest men in Texas. The kind who will shoot a man because of the way he parts his hair, because they don't like his shirt. They are land-pirates, Chase, ready for war at any moment. If there's money to be had they'll be armed, mounted and gone in no time. They make the big strikes, murder without giving it a second's thought, and feel no regret afterward.'

'Tucker, I. . . .' Chase protested again. Sweat was

trickling down his back, from under his arms, into his eyes where the gnats continued to pester him.

'That's where I'm taking you, kid. You see that? I am taking you to a very bad place. There are no laws, no conventions because that's the way they want it. I am the weakest of the lot, and you . . . you're only a pup, Chase. I wanted to tell you now because this is your last chance to turn around and hightail it out of here.'

'And where would I go, Tucker?' Chase Carver asked quietly. 'I'm riding with you. I trust you to keep me safe if we have to ride into hell through the front gate.'

'Which,' Tucker said with a sigh, 'is exactly where we are heading.'

THREE

It wasn't until late afternoon with the sun already reddening the long skies and purpling the thin scattered clouds which roofed the desert that they finally reached Bandolero. Ahead of them stretched a long dark mesa, low against the evening sky. It thrust itself against the darkness like a bulwark which, Tucker said, was exactly what it was.

'There's no way of approaching without being visible for miles around. Civilization ends at its edge.'

'I can see that. It's isolated enough,' Chase said a little uneasily. The formidable landform which bulked larger as they approached was no place a lawman – or an army – would feel comfortable approaching.

'Bandolero itself is at the foot of the mesa, on that projecting ledge,' Tucker said, indicating a shelf of rock extending a half-mile or so farther out into the desert. 'There is water there, seeping from the mesa. At the foot of the mesa there is graze for the horses because of the seep. They even keep a few head of cattle there. Once a man – I believe his name was Duncan – had a small, marginally successful little ranch up there. He's long gone now, of course.'

'What drove him off? Weather, Indians?'

'Some of both, I guess,' Tucker said vaguely. 'Anyway, when Kyle Jordan and Frank Butler were on the run, they found the place and forted up here. The posse chasing them didn't have a chance of dislodging them. Over the years a lot of other badmen drifted in, knowing they'd be welcome in Bandolero.'

'Butler and Jordan, should I know something about these men?' Chase asked as they approached the tongue of solid rock extending on to the flats. No men were visible; he saw no lights lit.

'Not beyond their names,' Tucker said. 'They are the boss dogs; that's all you need to know. It's better if you don't inquire about anyone's name or his business up there. I told you that before – I'm known but only tolerated up there. You – well, don't speak out of turn, don't look too long into any man's eyes; if you hear men laughing, don't join in, because another man might not find it so amusing. Don't take sides. Do your best to remain invisible and silent. With luck we won't be here long. And with luck we'll both leave alive and well.'

Chase nodded as Tucker found the foot of a rough trail and started the ascent toward the rocky shelf in the shadow of the bulking mesa. He knew that Tucker wasn't talking just to hear his own voice. Bandolero was a tough place, an outlaw town, inhabited by rougher men than any he had met on the cattle ranches in the mountains he knew. Those might laugh and happily go to work at trying to beat a man. The inhabitants of Bandolero would shoot a man down without passion, without compunctions.

'I've got the idea,' Chase said to Tucker. His voice was dry, his nerves were ajangle. The blue roan he rode plodded on, following Tucker's bay to the shelf of stone where the town of Bandolero stood waiting for him.

Cresting the rise, Chase got his first look at the outlaw town. A low line of buildings, all of native stone, stretched alone the foot of the mesa. Not far off to the left stood the remains of an old sawn-lumber house and barn. Duncan's original ranch buildings? There was a light in one of the upstairs windows of the unpainted, sagging building, and curtains in that window. Someone was living there. Chase had never met a man who hung curtains, and so he wondered. . . .

'Last building in the line is a stable,' Tucker said, gesturing to his right toward a stone building standing taller than the rest to accommodate a mounted man's passing. 'We'll put the ponies up for the night first. Then we'll just have a drink or two and listen to what's happening. But Chase. . . !'

'I know,' Chase said, 'I don't hear too much. I see less.'

'That's right,' Tucker said with relief. 'If you

33

happen to hear something – forget it. These men prize their secrets.'

'They can keep them. I just want to step out of leather and relax a little.'

With the horses put away, they walked through the gold and purple twilight to a second structure. This could only be a saloon. Rough talk, yelling, the sounds of glass breaking reached them before they made their way to the door of the stone building. Very narrow and very long, the low ceiling clotted with blue tobacco smoke.

Chase recoiled at the smell of the place as Tucker led the way through the door. The scent was of heavy tobacco, stale beer, sweaty men, and of something deeper which smelled vaguely like rotting fish. The men inside were broad-shouldered, heavily featured, and unyielding as Tucker and Chase tried to ease their way through them toward the bar.

Not a single man inside was not wearing a handgun, and many were decorated with two, and usually with a Bowie knife dangling from their belts. It was not a comfortable place to find oneself and Chase stumbled, staggered along, nudged on every side by shoulders and aggressive stances. No man moved aside even an inch for the two to pass, and bumping shoulders with one of the brutes could be construed as an insult or a challenge.

Chase, trying to weave his way through the crowd, looked up and met the gaze of a huge, bearded man. He quickly turned his eyes away. He did not intend to provide the man's entertainment on this evening. A gaunt, haggard man with a drooping mustache, the eyes of a watching predator, blocked his way. Chase stepped carefully around him, avoiding the wolfish eyes of the outlaw.

At length Tucker and Chase found a place on the far end of the scarred bar. Eyes continued to watch them – amused eyes, challenging eyes, disparaging eyes. Chase stared at the wood of the heavy bar, easing even closer to the stone wall next to where he found himself. He did not belong here, was not wanted here. A man jostled Chase roughly in the back, but Chase did not turn, did not even glance that way. There was a press of unwashed, heated bodies around him. Tucker had somehow ordered two glasses of whiskey and these were slapped down in front of them. Tucker was no less circumspect than Chase about observing the faces around them, but he did continue to glance up now and then, hopeful of seeing a friendly face, or at least one that was familiar.

'We'll have a couple more drinks just to let their curiosity fade a little,' Tucker whispered. 'Remember what I told you.'

The front door banged shut and Chase looked that way automatically as did almost everyone in the saloon. A bear of a man stood in the doorway. He had a shock of reddish hair and a zigzag scar running down his left cheek. He wore a black suit, black hat and white shirt without a tie. In his hand was a silver-tipped cane with a massive silver lion's

35

head. He marched into the room, the men parting before him deferentially. The giant paid most of them no attention. Chase heard muttered welcomes as he passed.

''Evening, Mr Jordan.'

'Howdy, Mr Jordan.'

So this was the legendary Kyle Jordan, one of the two men who had founded this robbers' roost which was now his feudal domain. Jordan elbowed up to the bar not far along, placed his cane down on the counter with a thump, and ordered whiskey. The men in his wake quieted down as if commanded by a common sense of reverence. Their king had arrived.

The red-haired man downed one whiskey and then another. Wiping his mouth almost daintily on the cuff of his shirt, he glanced around and his eyes fixed on Tucker. Jordan spoke up.

'On the dodge, Tucker?' his voice boomed.

'No, sir, Mr Jordan. Just thought I'd drift by and see how things were going down here.'

'Fine, fine. Good to see you again, Tucker.' Then he started talking with the wolfish man Chase had seen earlier. This outlaw was delivering what seemed to be an urgent bit of news, but Jordan only laughed, touched the man's shoulder and turned back to the bar.

'We'll be all right now,' Tucker told Chase. 'Kyle Jordan's vouched for us.' Tucker's manner was still tense; Chase's no less so. It was well and good that Jordan had spoken to Tucker, indicating to the rabble that Tucker was welcome here, but it did little to calm Chase's nerves. He wanted to be out of this outlaws' nest – the long empty desert had never seemed so appealing before.

'Think we'd better find some grub?' Chase asked as an excuse to leave more than anything else. It was true he had not eaten yet on this day, but his stomach's complaints were not so pressing at that moment as his need to get out of this place. Tucker only nodded, turning the whiskey glass in his hand thoughtfully.

'We'd better do that,' he agreed. 'We won't want to be here when the boys get good and drunk and start demonstrating how handy they are with their guns.'

They slipped away from the bar, Jordan ignoring them, and weaved their way again through the massed men to exit the saloon. Outside it was star-bright and cool, the air clean and pungent with the scent of sage.

'That's a relief,' Chas said as he followed Tucker down the street, away from the stink and clamor of the saloon.

'The boys are a bit tough,' Tucker said. 'What troubled me is I didn't see any of the old-time gang around.' He pondered silently for a minute. 'Could be they're all locked up or dead by now.'

'And that's how you have the edge of all of them,' Chase felt compelled to put in. 'Like you say; they aren't going to hang you or throw you in jail for skipping out on a hotel bill.'

Tucker almost smiled when he glanced at Chase. 'That's my theory, you have that right! It's better to be a live rat then a dead wolf.' He was silent again for a dozen strides. 'Sometimes though, I feel a little doubtful about my way of living. I haven't a chance of a big score to pad my old age. 'I'll probably be pulling the same petty grifts when I have a gray beard.'

'Well,' Chase responded as the smell of cooking lured them toward another gray stone building farther along the street, 'you'll be ahead of most of these men – how many of them are even going to see old age?'

Out of the corner of his eye Chase again noticed the lighted, curtained window in the old house that was set apart from the town proper on a low knoll. He asked Tucker about it: 'Who lives there?'

'What? Oh, St John,' Tucker replied.

Chase, not understanding, asked, 'Saint John?'

'Jeff St John. Him and his two daughters. I thought you'd've heard the name before.'

'Not me. Who is he?'

'He had him a nice little ranch down near Valentina, if you know where that is. Well one day the sheriff and three deputies came out to his ranch to tell St John he had better pay his taxes or he'd be thrown off his property. St John told the sheriff that he had damned sure paid his taxes and he would never stand for being chased off by the likes of him.

'The story was that the sheriff wanted the place for himself and he was lying about the taxes. Anyway things got rough for St John. One night someone set fire to his house. St John managed to kill two of the men before they rode off, but he couldn't save his wife who was trapped in a back room by the fire.

'St John was accused of murdering two county deputies, but he had already taken his two young daughters and headed for the Jeff Davis county line. There was a murder charge laid on him, of course. St John could probably have beaten it in another town, but Valentina was sewed up tight by the city hall crowd. St John was an outlaw and a desperate man, suddenly.'

Chase, who had been listening carefully, had only one question. 'Do you mean he lives up there with his two daughters? Here?'

'Well,' Tucker said as they reached the restaurant that had been their objective, 'he came here about ten years back, asking for nothing, ready to fight for a place to stay if he had to. Old Frank Butler and Kyle Jordan, they both kind of took to the man, so they let him have the old Butler house.'

'The daughters. . . ?'

'The less you know about them, the better. I thought you'd have learned your lesson about women. They come out now and again when things are fairly peaceful, but their father always comes with them, carrying his shotgun, and that twelve-gauge scattergun is always beside the front door of the house. I've told you, Chase, don't be so curious about things that aren't any of your concern.'

'A man likes to know where he's walking,' Chase

said. Tucker nodded.

'That's the only reason I told you.'

The restaurant was another of those square stone buildings set up against the base of the mesa. Full darkness had not yet settled, but the deep shadows cast by the brooding landform made things so gloomy that there was no difference. Inside the restaurant it was warm and scented with hot grease and frying beef. The building had a low ceiling with timbers showing, like the saloon they had just visited. The same men seemed to have built all of the buildings on the same plan. But then, Bandolero had been constructed for utility and not with design in mind.

The restaurant was not crowded at this hour. Of the twenty or so tables, only two were occupied. As he had been advised, Chase avoided eye contact with these men as Tucker led the way to a table against the wall not far from the kitchen door. He could hear the banging of heavy pots and pans being slung around in the kitchen. A broad man in a badly stained white apron emerged from within. Tucker asked Chase:

'Steak and fried potatoes all right with you?'

'Sure.'

The big man, his aims heavy with fur-like hair, scribbled down their order and pushed his way through the kitchen door. Chase glanced around. There were no curtains on the windows, no table-cloths on the rough tables. He realized what had been working at him. No woman was in evidence.

He tried to think if he had ever been in a restaurant before where there was not at least one woman.

He mentioned this to Tucker. The older man smiled and replied, 'No, Chase, women are hard to come by in Bandolero. Can't think of the last time I saw one. Now Toomey,' he said, nodding toward the big man who had taken their order, 'he once had himself an Indian woman, his wife, who worked here. She's long gone now.'

'She went back to her people?' Chase asked and Tucker frowned, scratching at his whiskered jaw.

'She just came up missing one day, Chase. Aren't you ever going to learn not to ask so many questions?'

Toomey was back with their platters. Slapping them down on the table he walked heavily away. Cutting a piece of tough, bloody steak, Chase asked another question. 'Tell me this, Tucker: this man Duncan who built the house St John now lives in, started a small ranch up here before Jordan and Butler rode in. Did the Indians, the hard weather drive him out . . . or did he just come up missing one day as well?'

'Son,' Tucker said around a mouthful of food, 'it seems you just don't want to learn. 'I'll tell you anything you need to know, but don't go around asking questions that don't concern you.'

They ate silently after that. A few patrons came in or left, banging the badly hung door shut.

Chase could feel Tucker's disapproval throughout the supper, though the older man said nothing further. When the big man, Toomey, came to collect, Tucker handed over silver money without hesitation. Bandolero was no place to try grifting. Chase looked at the man's furry paw as he collected the money, then once at his mean, slack-jowled face, wondering if Toomey had caused his Indian wife to disappear, and how.

Outside once again, Tucker lit his pipe. Chase's eyes studied the distant sliver of a golden moon rising over the desert flats, glanced at the now-unlit window of the house of Jeff St John, wondering about the girls who lived there. Girls? They must be young women by now, isolated in this desert hideout, surrounded by bandits. He shook his thoughts aside.

'Where to now?' he asked Tucker.

'We find us some beds – unless you want to go back to the saloon for some entertainment.' Tucker's voice was sly, and Chase took the words for the jest they had been.

'No, I don't feel up to that kind of fun,' Chase said. As he spoke, an echoing pistol shot sounded in the saloon or near it. He could see several men, pistols in their hands, racing toward the front door of the place. The men around here had odd ways of amusing themselves, it seemed. 'Where?' Chase asked, looking down the street.

'That last building in the line is old Charlie Knight's place. He'll rent me a room.' They walked on through the warm evening. 'Old Charlie, he's a friend of mine. Used to be a hellraiser in his time.

Took a bullet in the hip down in El Paso. Now he just sits by the fire and waits for the sun to come up or the sun to go down, counting the hours.'

Tucker spoke reflectively. Perhaps the old outlaw saw a similar end for himself.

The small, square, stone building was a replica of most of the others. It did have a wooden porch in front, an awning of pole construction over it. There was a cane rocking chair on the porch, presumably where Charlie Knight liked to sit and watch the sun rise.

They were about to step up on to the porch when there was a crash inside the building, and a hurried rush toward the door with accompanying muffled cursing. Tucker stepped back immediately and Chase drew away from the door as well.

Three men rushed through the door, or rather, two men tried to rush out – the third was held between them and was being dragged forcibly from the place, kicking and screaming. Throwing this one into the street, the two men began kicking him, punching him, laughing all the time.

Chase saw at once that their victim was no more than his own age. The two attackers had yanked him so that their prey had been hoisted up by his collar, and now, on his knees, the young man tried futilely to avoid the punches raining down upon him. Chase stepped that way; Tucker's restraining hand gripped his arm. The younger man was moaning, crying out now for mercy, but he was getting none. Fists continued to batter his face and body.

Then by the dull illumination of the rising moon and the scant starlight, Chase saw the glint of steel as one of the roughnecks drew a savage-looking bowie knife from its sheath. Chase could hold himself back no longer. He tore his arm free of Tucker's grip and strode toward the tussle. As the man with the bowie drew it back to strike, Chase slammed the heavy barrel of his Colt revolver against the attacker's wrist. The sound of bone cracking was loud in the night, and the thug cried out in pain, dropping his knife, holding his broken hand. His friend looked up in puzzlement, in anger, and started to draw his handgun.

'I'll blow you away,' Chase Carver warned him. 'Get away from here. Get his wrist tended to.'

'You'll pay,' the outlaw snarled in a guttural voice.

'Likely. But if you don't get out of here now, you'll pay a lot sooner.' As Chase was saying that, he eased back the hammer of his blue-steel Colt. Neither of the bruisers was willing to take matters any further. They backed away, the man with the broken wrist assisted by his partner.

'Thanks, mister,' the man on the ground said, struggling to get to his feet. His words were a shallow pant. There was blood in his eye and a stream of it trickling from his ear. His jaw was swelling. His movements were unsteady. Tucker stretched out an arm and helped him to stand. The young man stood there swaying on his feet, as if he were on the hurricane deck of a ship during a storm.

'Are you all right?' Chase asked.

'I will be,' the young man promised. 'They were going to beat me to death, mister. I thank you for what you did. If you ever need anything in the world, you just ask me – Dan Quick – and I'll be there to help you.'

Then he staggered away, looking none too well. Chase didn't have to turn around to know that Tucker's eyes were boring into him furiously. Still, Tucker said nothing as Chase returned to the door of the building, holstering his gun.

Chase said in frustration, 'What else was I to do! They were going to kill the man.' When the scowling Tucker didn't answer, Chase added, 'At least I've made a friend.'

'Yeah,' Tucker allowed, 'you've made one friend – and two blood enemies.'

FOUR

The night passed restlessly. After midnight the room in the stone house grew cold. Tucker had not said a word to Chase after the hobbling Charlie Knight had showed them to their beds. Chase had tried to draw Tucker out, to apologize, but with no result. The old outlaw was miffed – and more.

Chase knew what he had done wrong; mixed into other men's affairs in Bandolero. But Dan Quick's assailants would have beaten the young man to death. Chase couldn't have lived with himself if he had just stood by and let that happen. Let Tucker be mad!

Chase realized that the two men would come back looking for him. He also knew that he had drawn Tucker into the mess, but what else was he to have done?

He rolled over in his bed, drawing the thin blanket Knight had provided up tight beneath his chin. Tomorrow, perhaps, he should just ride off and leave Tucker – for the old outlaw's protection.

46

Just saddle his little blue roan and ride . . . where? He knew nothing of this part of the country, nothing of Texas, had little prospect of finding work. He might well find himself back in an alley somewhere fighting with Texas dogs over kitchen scraps.

He did not sleep more than two or three hours on that night. Nevertheless he was up before Tucker, who still lay curled in his bed as Chase stamped into his boots to greet the morning. It was dark and cool in the stone house, bright and cool outside. Charlie Knight sat in his rocking chair, watching the red sun rise and color the far skies. The old man glanced up languidly and nodded to Chase.

'It's how our lifetimes pass, sunup to sundown,' he muttered, indicating the colored eastern sky.

'Yes, sir,' Chase answered, at a loss for a response.

Chase perched on the edge of the porch, watching the sunrise for a while. Almost without thought he let his eyes drift to the wooden house on the knoll – the old Duncan place where St John and his two daughters had taken up residence. Charlie Knight noticed this but made no comment. Instead he did say:

'I thank you for pulling Dan Quick's fat out of the fire. He's a good boy, just a little green.'

Like me, Chase thought.

'I guess Dan told you about the work to be done over at St John's,' Knight said.

'No, sir, we didn't really have that much time to

47

talk,' Chase answered, not knowing what the old man was referring to.

'Well, maybe he'll be by later to talk to you. If he hasn't decided to take to his heels and hie out of here now that the Boyer brothers are out to get him.'

'Was that who it was, last night? Why do they want to get Dan?' Chase asked.

'He made 'em mad,' was the terse reply. There was a crackle in Charlie Knight's words which might have been taken for a laugh. Chase reflected that again he had violated Bandolero's etiquette – he had asked another question about matters that didn't concern him. He supposed he would never learn the way of the outlaws.

'Speak of the devil,' Charlie Knight said, jabbing a horny finger uptown. Chase turned his head and saw the lanky, shambling figure of Dan Quick approaching them, hat tugged low, fresh bandages on his face. He also wore a six-gun, which looked ready for use. He had apparently been taken unaware the night before. Having been unarmed then, he seemed intent on making sure it did not happen again.

Quick approached the two men on the porch, his eyes shifting from point to point. His movements were uncertain and uneasy. Charlie Knight called out:

'They ain't around anywhere! Probably still sleeping it off.' Again the dry cackle emerged from his throat. Knight was seemingly amused by the timid-

48

ity of today's would-be outlaws.

'Good,' was all Quick had to say, though his eyes showed deep relief. It was obvious that he was in no hurry to meet the Boyer brothers again. He propped a boot up on the stone step of the building's porch and nodded to Chase Carver. 'I'm glad to find you here,' he said, extending a hand. He and Chase exchanged names, and Quick went on, 'I suppose you've heard that I need a little help on this job I'm doing today?'

Quick was looking at Charlie, who shook his head negatively. Chase shrugged his ignorance. 'No – well then, I'll tell you what it is.'

Chase waited with some trepidation. Did Quick want to rob a bank somewhere or to avenge himself against the Boyer brothers? It was nothing so dramatic.

'St John – do you know who he is? – chimney finally caved in. No wonder, the thing must be fifty years old, and made of stone, of course. It's hard to fit stone into a strong, straight form, even for a mason. And Butler was no mason; and of course Butler didn't even have concrete to work with, so it was mostly held together with adobe mud and a prayer. I guess stones have been falling off the thing for years, and finally it's gone all to hell. Want to give me a hand patching it up, Chase?'

Tucker had not mentioned any plans, and would probably welcome a day apart from his young protégé. Chase, himself, had no other plans. What was there to do in Bandolero?

49

'Of course,' he told Quick. 'Be happy to help, though I'm no mason either.'

'Neither am I,' Dan said with a smile, 'but we've got to be able to make things better than they are for the old brute.'

'I thought he didn't let anyone come near his house,' Chase said.

'He doesn't, but what's a man to do – he's too old and fat to go up a ladder and do this sort of work.'

'How'd you get the job?' Chase asked out of curiosity.

'Last year his well got fouled and he hired me to clean it out. He noticed that I worked at it all day in the hot sun, didn't overcharge him – and didn't even try to peek at his daughters. I guess you'd say the old man trusts me now.'

'Should he?' Chase asked playfully, getting to his feet, and Dan only laughed.

'Well, I'll put it this way – I sure respect that shotgun he always carries. He's not a man to cross.'

On foot the two men walked up the gradual slope, approaching the St John house. Dan asked casually, 'What kind of paper do you have out on you, Chase?'

'I don't get your meaning,' Chase replied. Distantly they could hear a deep-throated dog barking as they neared the house.

Dan looked surprised. It was already warm and a trickle of perspiration had escaped from the sweatband of his hat to trickle across his forehead. 'Why, I mean what sort of warrants do you have?' the young outlaw said.

'Warrants? I haven't any,' Chase said, watching the weather-aged, two-story house ahead, studying the upstairs window where he had seen a light burning behind the curtains the night before.

'Really,' Dan said in surprise. 'So they never tied you into anything, huh? You're a lucky man, I guess.'

'I suppose,' Chase answered, continuing to plod up the hill with his eyes on the house ahead. They were raising dust in their passage, and the breeze was at their backs drifting it over them. 'I never have committed any crime, if that's what you mean.'

'A virgin among us!' Dan said with a tight laugh. 'Then tell me – why in hell are you here in Bandolero?'

Chase didn't feel like unraveling the whole story for Dan. 'I just sort of got tangled up with Tucker. He brought me here.'

'I'll be damned,' Dan laughed. 'So there is one innocent man in Bandolero!' His eyes said,

The way you tell it.

They came upon a badly hung gate in the middle of a misaligned picket fence dropping scales of white paint along its length. The house ahead seemed dark, crooked as if the desert had invaded its supports and sapped the strength from them. The shingled roof was missing many wooden scabs. The chimney, Chase saw at once, was badly in need of repair if not replacement. Standing at the south side of the house, there were chunks of stone

51

missing from it, spilled across the roof or dropped to the ground at its base. No windows, no door stood open in the front of the house. Chase stretched out a hand to open the gate, but Dan halted him sharply.

'No! Don't even touch that gate until Jeffrey St John comes out and allows it.' Chase let his hand slide away from the latch.

'He's a careful man,' Chase said. 'Does all of that come from fear for his daughters' safety?'

'Most of it – although a man living around Bandolero has a lot of reasons to be cautious.'

'Are his daughters . . . attractive?' Chase asked and Dan laughed. 'They are, my friend. But you'd better be wary of even glancing their way. I met them when I was cleaning out the well for St John. He didn't even like a casual word or two passing between me and his daughters.'

'What are they like?' Chase asked, wondering how the two young women liked living in a barricaded fortress surrounded by outlaws.

'The older one, her name's Christine, is tall and moves like a cat,' Dan said. 'I mean, she has long legs, a demure manner – if that's the right word – shy of men and suspicious of them. I guess that's a part of her father. Now Louise!' Dan laughed and explained.

'She's generally called "Lou" or "Lulu" by her sister when Christine's teasing her. She's tall and pretty as well. Long black hair and black eyes, but man! She is a regular hellcat. She starts out by yelling at a man and then gets more pugnacious. Like a cat stuffed into a bag, Louise is. I suppose that's a part of her father, too,' Dan said thoughtfully, 'or of her life here, which can't be much more fun than being in jail.'

Chase only nodded; he supposed that was a natural reaction to being locked away and strictly raised – although he could understand St John's motives as well. Bandolero was no place for a woman of any stripe.

'What do we do now?' he asked Dan.

'Start yelling, "Hallo the house!" and wait for the old brute to come out and let us on to his property.'

They stood together for long minutes, hailing the house as the breeze that had risen with the morning sun drifted red dust over them. Finally, the heavy door at the front of the house opened and St John emerged. Chase saw a portly man with only a few strands of dark hair swept across his balding dome. He wore knee-high boots, and on this morning a coat and vest without a shirt. His shotgun was held familiarly in his hands. Chase uttered a small surprised sound. Dan restrained a smile with effort.

'He's a beauty, isn't he?' Dan commented.

What he was, Chase thought, was a man who had been dealt a rough hand by fate and had played it badly. With his wife dead and his property confiscated he was living in forced isolation in an outlaw town trying to raise two daughters. His eyes, as he approached, were heavily bagged and quite sad, though his perpetual suspicion of outsiders showed in them.

Those eyes were dark, but milky as if his vision was not too good. A sort of pleased smile tinged with surprise loosened his small mouth into a sort of smile as he recognized Dan Quick.

'Danny,' St John said with a voice that was relieved and distantly welcoming.

'Come to see about your chimney, Mr St John. This is my helper, Chase Carver.'

St John's smile flattened out as he studied Chase. 'Figure you need an assistant on the job, Dan?'

'Yes, sir, I do.'

'Well. . . .' St John said unhappily. 'I suppose it's all right – but I won't pay more for two men than for one. Money's tight.'

'That's all right,' Dan said, smiling boyishly. 'We agreed on a price, and that's fine.'

'Then I guess I'd better let you get to it,' St John said, swinging the gate inward. He growled a little as the rusty hinges complained. He seemed to have another thought in mind, but he subdued it. Chase thought the fat man had probably briefly considered asking Dan if he could fix the fence, but realized that it would cost him money to have the job done. How did St John even manage to support his family as it was?

Following St John toward the house, Chase found himself continuing to watch the curtained upstairs room. He supposed it was natural, but he felt vaguely ashamed of himself for his interest in the two sisters.

St John pointed out the obvious flaws in his chimney and the fallen stonework littering the roof and yard, and waved a hand toward the nearby barn.

'All the tools I have are in there – somewhere. There's also a ladder,' he told them. 'Try to get finished today, if you can.'

'We'll do our best,' Dan promised. St John stood looking at Dan's battered face for a moment, shook his head with unspoken remonstrance, and shuffled away toward the house. From somewhere the still-unseen deep-throated dog continued to voice its disapproval of strangers on the property.

'Clean up the fallen stone first,' Quick said. 'Pile it to one side and we'll see if we can make it into something. I sure hope so,' he added. 'I'd hate to think we have to quarry new stone.'

Chase flinched at that sobering thought as well. He was no mason, and he damned sure was no quarryman. Nevertheless, now that he was here he meant to give the job his best. It was already growing hot in this desert corner of Texas, and Chase placed his gunbelt on a nail protruding from the side of the barn and began unbuttoning his shirt, meaning to place it aside as well.

'No,' Dan told him sharply. 'Not with the two girls around. St John will have a fit if he sees you without a shirt.'

Chase said nothing, but began buttoning his shirt again. He was unfamiliar with rules like that, but if that was the way things were, he was willing to follow Dan's advice. 'What do you want me to do?' he asked Quick.

'We'll get the ladder and then you can clear off whatever's fallen to the roof. Start a pile nearby. I'll try to find where St John's been getting his adobe mortar from and mix it up in whatever container I can find – though I wish we had cement. The weather's going to get bad again come winter, and the adobe will wash away just as it did before.'

'But it will last another few years, won't it?'

'With luck. All we can do is the best we can with what we have.'

Chase stood looking up into the bright sky toward the roof of the house. He nodded. 'Let's find that ladder.'

They recovered the splintered, unstable ladder from the barn in minutes. While Dan probed around among the zinc tubs and barrows looking for something to mix his adobe mortar in, Chase carried the ladder back to the house, placed it next to the broken chimney, and climbed it somewhat unsteadily to the pitched roof of the house.

There was a litter of dislodged stones across the roof. Some had rolled off to the ground, others lay where they had landed. Chase had picked out a spot in the yard below where he meant to stack the usable rock, and he began lugging them that way, tossing them on to the pile. There was no sign of Dan, and anyway Quick knew what he was up to, so Chase had no concerns about hitting his new-found friend with the rocks, which after an hour or so at his task, he began to hurl more confidently, if not recklessly, in the direction of the stone pile.

The sun grew hot on his back; perspiration trickled into his eyes, stinging them. It was through sweat-blurred vision that he saw the unexpected, almost spectral figure of a young woman clinging to the top of the ladder, peering up over the eaves at him.

'Hey you!' the apparition shouted. 'What are you trying to do, knock me on the head?'

FIVE

'Hello,' Chase said, holding out a hand to help the slender young woman in jeans and long-sleeved white shirt on to the roof. He wiped at his brow and stood gazing at her for a moment. 'You must be Louise.'

'I am.' She seemed a little surprised. Sitting down on the slanted roof she asked, 'How did you know?'

Somewhat sheepishly Chase sat beside the dark-haired girl and said, 'Well, Dan Quick described the only two girls around to me, and you didn't match the impression I had of Christine.'

'Oh? How'd he describe Christine?'

'Different from you,' Chase said, trying for politeness.

'Well, she is, Danny couldn't have been very kind in speaking about me.' She had picked up a small chunk of rock. Now she winged it in the vicinity of the stack of stones below. 'I don't like Danny,' she said.

'Why not?'

'Well, I suppose it's because he likes my sister – I don't know. He's hot for her, you know?'

'I don't even know what you mean,' Chase said, again drawing his cuff across his perspiring forehead.

'You must – you're a man,' Louise said.

'Well, I don't – exactly,' Chase answered hesitantly.

Louise had noticed Chase wiping at his brow. 'It's so hot up here, why don't you take your shirt off?'

'I was told that wouldn't go over so well with your father.'

'Probably not,' Louise said, nibbling on her lower lip. 'But if Danny Quick said it, he probably just didn't want Christine to see you with your shirt off.'

Chase laughed out loud. 'It wouldn't be any terrific sight.'

'I didn't say it would be,' Louise said in a voice which was low and mocking. 'I just said that Danny might think that way.'

'Anyway, I'm about ready to go back down. I've got to pick up the large stones down in the yard.' He added, 'I'm sorry if I almost hit you.'

'That's all right,' Louise said, standing as he did. 'It wasn't really that close, and it's my own fault for coming out while you were working. I was looking for our dog – he bolted out the door when Father came back in, and wouldn't come when he was called. He knows Dan, of course, and you were up on the roof, but Bobo does bite.'

'Bobo?'

'Bobo. You'll know him if you see him – he's big and black and always has his hackles up. He has a mean temper. I think that's why Father keeps him around.'

'To guard his daughters?'

'Well, I guess so.' She led the way to the ladder. The wind had increased and it pressed her shirt prettily against her body. 'You'd have to understand a little about our background – or did Dan fill you in on that too?' she asked as they descended.

'He did,' Chase admitted and added drily, 'and I've met some of the men in this town.'

'A charming group, aren't they?' Louise said, frowning tightly. 'That's why Christine is so desperate to escape from Bandolero.'

'With Dan?' Chase said in amazement.

'There's no one else, is there? If only . . . well, Dan has no money.'

'I thought not – why else would he be taking this kind of job? Except to see Christine, of course.'

'Of course,' Louise said. Chase saw a blur of black fur rushing toward him, hackles stiffly risen along a broad spine. He withdrew a step or two – his success with dogs had not been that good lately. Louise silenced the snarling dog with a single sharp word and it slunk away.

'Bobo?' Chase asked.

'Bobo.' She looked one way and then the other and said, 'I'd better let you get back to work.'

Chase nodded and watched as she strode slowly away. Then he got to work gathering the fallen stones that were spread out across the yard. By the time he had finished that, Dan was back with a wheelbarrow full of reddish-brown adobe mud. Placing it down, he mixed the mortar a little more with a hoe.

'I put some lime in it,' Dan said. 'I thought it might make it stronger.'

Chase only nodded dubiously. He had no idea if lime would strengthen the mortar. He thought that it was used in concrete, but he had never mixed that either. He figured it didn't matter; this was Dan's project, and it was up to him to make the decisions.

'I wish we knew which rocks were where in the first place,' Dan said as he looked up at the dilapidated chimney. 'No way of knowing that, of course. We'll just use the biggest ones at the base of the thing and work our way up, hoping we don't run out.'

'We shouldn't, should we?'

'Some might have fallen inside the house,' Dan reminded him, 'or just been thrown aside out here if they got in someone's way.'

'Bobo might have been playing with some of them,' Chase said and Dan laughed.

'You've met Bobo, then?'

'Not formally. I think he would have liked to tear my leg off if Louise hadn't been here.'

Dan's eyes narrowed. 'Lou? Out here?'

'She said that she wanted to put the dog in the house so it didn't make any trouble for us,' Chase told him.

'I see,' Dan said. He glanced at the sun. 'We'd better get started, Chase. At about noon that sun's going to blister us.'

The work was slow and arduous as are all jobs when a man doesn't really know what he's doing. Rocks were set in place, fell off again. It would take days for the adobe to dry. Duncan, or whoever it was that had first built the chimney, had obviously taken his time, laying a tier at a time. That was the only way it could be done properly. Chase and Dan had not the luxury of time. St John wanted the job done today – perhaps partly because he did not want two young men lingering in his daughters' presence.

By noon it was well over a hundred degrees. The stones were hot on their fingers. Sweat trickled down their bodies. There was no shade on this side of the house; the sun merely reflected hotly off the wall. Still, they were making some progress. The rebuilt chimney was nearly to the top of the second story. They worked very carefully now, not wanting the whole experiment to collapse on them.

She came around the corner of the house wearing a blue dress and a red ribbon in her dark hair. She carried a tray with a pitcher of lemonade and two glasses on it. Dan straightened up immediately as if embarrassed and excited at once. Chase needed no one to introduce Christine St John to him. Who else could she be?

Her long legs moved smoothly beneath the light fabric of her summer dress. Her shoulders were square and slightly wide, suggesting an athletic body. Her face was oval and was made mysteriously attractive by her sapphire-blue eyes which flanked a nose with a hint of an arch. Her mouth was generous, with a full underlip.

In her eyes Chase read what could be haughtiness or only the sort of uncertainty that makes some people develop a kind of defensive shyness. She was not shy with Dan Quick, although she barely glanced at Chase, which was fine with him. Comparing St John's two daughters, he found himself preferring Louise – as if it mattered one way or the other.

'You boys must be awfully thirsty,' Christine said. 'I'd invite you up on to the front porch to sit in the shade a while, but. . . .' But St John would certainly frown on making a social occasion out of this job.

Christine glanced at the half-completed chimney. 'It seems you're making headway. It was kind of you, Danny, to do this for Father.'

'He's paying us,' Dan said. He took a glass of lemonade and handed the other to Chase. Chase Carver moved carefully away from them, toward the scant shade of the eaves of the barn. The two were doing a lot more speaking with their eyes than with their lips; still Chase caught a phrase or two here and there as the dry wind twisted past. He looked toward the desolate outlaw town below as a shot rang out from somewhere.

Christine was saying, 'If only . . . but where would we. . . ?'

63

Dan answered in rapid, wind-interrupted sentences. 'As soon as I . . . I promise you, Christine . . . you know how I. . . .'

It was not the sort of conversation Chase wished to overhear even if it were possible to make out their words and promises. He had held such secret meetings with Laura Wheaton up at the Timberline not so long ago. What followed had been humiliation, banishment, and near-starvation. He doubted that Dan would have much more luck with Jeffrey St John than he himself had had with Moss Wheaton.

After a few minutes Christine St John whisked herself away without waiting for Chase to return his glass to the tray she carried. Approaching Dan, Chase found his new-found friend's face dark with displeasure. Chase said:

'Well, the lemonade hit the spot.'

Dan only grunted a response. He was in no mood for it. His eyes watched an indefinite distant spot, maybe the last point at which he had seen Christine's retreating back. Chase placed a hand briefly on his shoulder.

'We'd better get back to work if we're going to finish this today.'

'Who cares!' Dan exploded. 'Tell me, Chase – is it always the money, only the money?'

'I wouldn't know. I've never had any,' Chase answered, reaching for a large rock he thought he had spotted a place for.

'That's what I mean,' Dan said, 'Neither have I. But I mean to go out and get some!'

The two rested that evening at a far corner table in the saloon as men trickled in and went out again. Outside, twilight had settled and the sky had gone to a pleasant cool purple. One star showed through the murk of sundown color.

'Well, have you made up your mind yet?' Dan said. He had just taken his third shot of whiskey. Chase himself had taken two, and although he was developing no taste for the stuff, he was starting to enjoy the effects of the raw spiuits. He felt bolder, more reckless. He did not turn his eyes away from the hard glares of the outlaws who crowded the tables, drinking.

'Made up my mind?' Chase replied. 'About what?'

'Chase, you heard me talking about finding a way to make some money – enough to change my life.'

'I heard you, but I thought you were just talking to yourself.'

Dan leaned forward, clasping his hands together on the table. There was a tension in the man that could be felt. He had been that way since they had left St John's property.

'I mean to include you in,' Dan said. 'I'll need a partner.' He leaned back again, let his eyes flicker around the room and added, 'You and me, Chase, we're in the same boat.'

'How do you mean?' Chase asked through narrowed eyes. The warmth the whiskey had started in his stomach seemed to have risen to his head as well.

'What do I mean?' Dan laughed. 'Look at us! You've seen the way I'm treated in this town. And you! How do you plan on surviving? You've got no job, no money. You're just dragging around, living off an old petty grifter's handouts. And how long can that last? He'll get tired of it sooner or later.'

'Tucker has helped me out,' Chase said. 'He's been trying to show me a few ways to get along.'

'As well as he does!' Dan, who was getting fairly loud, laughed again. 'And you see how they treat him as well in Bandolero. What's next? Is he going to teach you how to rob the poor box in a church? Look, Chase, you have two things in the world you can count on – you've got that nice pony of yours . . . and you've got a Colt revolver.

'The horse can't make much for you, in fact it'll cost you – you have to feed it. That sidearm of yours, however, can help you to make some real money.' He lifted his eyes sharply. 'Or have you already forgotten about this Laura Wheaton of yours? Throw in with me. We can make some money,' Dan said intently.

'I'm no thief, Dan.'

'Everyone's a thief!' Quick countered, gesturing for more whiskey. 'It's just that some folks know how to go about it right and others don't. Look, is it your ambition to become a petty thief like Tucker, scraping by between stays in jail? You don't get rich; you don't get any respect.' His voice lowered again.

'You'll never have a woman, not of the kind you want.'

There was a minor ruckus at the bar and three men trooped through the door. Two of them were wearing leather chaps. They meant to do some rough riding somewhere. Chase asked Dan, 'Who's that?'

'Russ Proctor, John Knight, Willie Lynch. I've heard about it – as much as these boys claim to keep their lips tight, when they start drinking they can't help but start talking. See, they're careless – not like me. They're planning on riding over to Kent and emptying the bank there.'

'Sounds dangerous,' Chase said, picking up his fresh shot of whiskey.

'Of course it is! But that's the challenge of it. Besides, if it all goes right, they'll all have a year's worth of cash to live off. Of course they'll waste it. And they'll have to pay tribute to Kyle Jordan and Frank Butler.'

'How's that?'

'You didn't know about that? Sure, Jordan and Butler own this town and they require that everyone give them a split of their take when they pull a job for the privilege of having a safe haven to return to. Yeah,' Dan muttered, 'those two are the only ones in Bandolero who will ever die rich.'

'I guess it's fair,' Chase said, 'depending on how you look at it.'

'Anyway,' Dan said, slapping down his empty shot glass. 'That's what those three are up to. So what do you say, Chase, are you ready to ride with me or not?'

The whiskey continued to buzz in Chase's brain. He had become a different man under its influence. Was Dan Quick proposing a stick-up? Was Chase seriously considering going along with him? He thought briefly of Laura Wheaton, far away, perhaps thinking that someday Chase Carver would return for her, about how much land he could buy with a few dollars up in Timberline, how little it would cost to build a cabin with all of the tall pines growing there.

'Are you talking about traveling with Knight and Lynch?' he asked in a raw whisper. Dan's face seemed oddly blurred across the table.

'Hell no!' Dan erupted. 'I wouldn't ask them and they wouldn't take us along if I did.' He leaned nearer again. 'But I've got something in mind that requires us to ride out shortly after they do. And I think it's better we prepare now, before we have any more to drink, while we've still got some of St John's change to buy provisions.'

Dan rose as the bank robbers exited the building. 'Let's do it, Chase – or are you going to wait around and see if Tucker is going to put up with you for a little while longer?'

'But what. . . ?'

'Stand up and be a man with me or trot around after that old cheap chiseler, Tucker. That's your two choices. My way there's a good chance we'll both make the money we need to be with the women we want.'

Chase stood, hesitating. Dan Quick was spinning out dreams, Chase knew that. He also knew that Dan was speaking the truth about his chances with Tucker. And the old man had shown that he was already impatient with his student. Tucker had found him when he was down, pulled him to his feet, fed him and put a horse under him, but why should Chase expect him to do more?

Tucker had shown him the path. Now, it seemed it was time for Chase Carver to make his own way along the trail.

Even if was the outlaw trail.

SIX

Chase and Dan Quick followed the gang of bank robbers out of Bandolero so closely that they could see their dust drifting, smell it in the air. Dan held back a little, saying, 'We'd better not get too close on their heels, they might think we're up to something.'

'Well, aren't we?'

'Yes, but it has nothing to do with them – not directly. And John Knight and Willie Lynch are both sudden men with a gun – they wouldn't wait for conversation.'

Chase nodded silently and followed along on the night trail riding behind Dan, toward the rising moon. The moon drew shadows across the rocky earth beneath the cactus and stands of sage. It was a still night, growing rapidly cooler. Chase turned to look back in the direction of Bandolero, but he saw nothing but the massive bulk of the mesa. There was no sign that anyone lived up there. He realized that he had been hopeful, futilely, of seeing the St John house. He thought briefly of Louise's bright eyes and merry little smile. There was nothing to prompt these thoughts – just idle ideas a man has along the trail.

There was plenty to sustain his thoughts of Laura Wheaton. A kiss in the moonlight, her hand brushing against his cheek, promises spoken.

Would she have changed her mind by the time he returned to her? Finding a solution to his problems seemed suddenly urgent. Almost as urgent as Dan's determination to get rich quick and rescue Christine from what must be a prison to her. She lived surrounded by outlaws, rough men kept at bay only by her father's shotgun and a wild-eyed dog. Dan Quick, such as he was, must have seemed to be a sort of savior to Christine, a man who promised a better future for her.

But what was it Dan had in mind, exactly? Earlier in the evening Chase had let himself be convinced that there was something to this, some good to come of it. Right now, as the liquor he had drunk began to clear away, he could not recall what their plan was – if Dan had even told him. He nudged the little blue roan with his knees and eased up to ride beside Dan Quick.

'It looks like they're veering off to the east a little,' Chase said, indicating the dust which still lifted into the night skies from the passing of the horses of Proctor, Knight and Lynch. Dan nodded. 'I know it. We're not traveling that way. I just wanted to be behind them so that we could time our move properly.'

71

'What move is that?' Chase wanted to know.

'Well it's pretty simple, a little risky, and depends on how those boys fare.'

'Do you want to tell it to me plain?' Chase asked. He was feeling a little sour, and now his head had begun to develop a slow throbbing ache. 'I think I've the right to know.'

'Of course you do!' Dan glanced around as if they were still sitting in a saloon where listeners could overhear his plan. 'Where are those boys going?' he asked, nodding in the direction Proctor and his crew had taken.

'Well, you told me that they planned to rob the bank at Kent this morning.'

'That's exactly it. Kent is a small town. All they've got for a town marshal is an old pensioner. They figure it for a safe enough job, and it is. But they won't get much out of the bank in a town that size.'

'Then, why. . . ?' Chase tried to ask, but Dan didn't let himself be interrupted.

'What's going to happen as soon as the bank is robbed? They'll wire to the Culberson County sheriff over in Van Horn, the county seat. The county sheriff – Will Bigsby is his name – will have no choice but to gather his deputies and whoever else he can find for a posse and ride after them. And he'll have a fair idea of where they're heading – back to Bandolero.'

'I don't see. . . .' Chase tried again, His head was throbbing badly now. The saddle beneath him seemed to jolt roughly with each step of the roan.

He vowed to forgo whiskey for the rest of his life.

'What happens then?' Dan asked confidently. Chase had no idea. He shook his head heavily. Dan explained, 'With the sheriff and his deputies, and maybe half of the able-bodied men in Van Horn hotfooting to cut off the Kent bank robbers, the bank in Van Horn will be an easy target.'

'That's where we're going?'

'You are so right!' Dan said proudly.

'Van Horn's a bigger town, isn't it?'

'It is, and that means the bank in Van Horn has a lot more money in it than those boys are going to get out of the job in Kent.'

'There's only the two of us, Dan,' Chase cautioned, but Quick was in a reckless mood.

'A man alone has been known to stick up a bank, Chase. It's just that two makes it more certain.' He spoke in a confiding voice. 'What we are going to do is post up on the outskirts of Van Horn – it'll take a little while for the sheriff to get the word and summon his deputies – then when we see a posse riding out of Van Horn, we ride in and take care of our own business.'

The way Dan told it, it seemed as simple as picking peaches, but Chase rode on in silence, wondering how he had ever gotten himself into something like this. After an hour or so he did manage to ask:

'Dan? Have you ever been involved in anything like this before?'

'No, I never have. But there's a first time for

73

everything, Chase!' He still spoke confidently, apparently pleased with himself for having come up with this scheme. Chase Carver rode on through the dismal night, thinking about one thing Dan had said: There's a first time for everything.

Sure there was. There was also always a first time for dying.

They camped on a low, brushy knoll on the outskirts of Van Horn, Texas. Briefly they slept, then rose to sit watching the town for hours as the sun emerged from its night hiding place and bled red light across the far skies. Below them Van Horn sprawled across the plains. It was even bigger than Chase had expected. That didn't seem to trouble Dan. He sat patiently watching the town, his knees drawn up, arms looped around them.

'It's that green building facing the street,' he said. There was a sort of excited quiver in his voice, an unnatural brightness in his eyes. Chase felt no excitement. His stomach churned, his head ached. He had gotten himself caught up in another man's scheme which he had no heart for.

'What do we do?' he asked Dan in a weak voice.

'For now we just wait,' Dan said, leaning back on his elbows.

An hour passed, and another. 'They won't hit the bank in Kent until it opens,' he said. 'That ought to be happening pretty soon. When it's done, someone will send a wire to Sheriff Bigsby. It won't be long now and things will start popping.'

74

But it was long. Chase sat on the brushy knoll, staring at the town below. Nothing happened. There was no movement anywhere except for Dan who had checked the loads in his revolver at least three times. There was that and a red ant which made its way through the tiny forest of the hairs on the back of Chase's hand. Abruptly, Dan sat up, his muscles tensing.

'Here we go,' he said.

Squinting into the sunlight, Chase could see nothing which might have triggered Dan's interest. All he saw was a boy of twelve or thirteen running down the street toward a squat adobe structure two blocks away from the bank building.

'Telegraph boy, I'll wager,' Dan said getting to his feet. 'Running to the sheriff's office. It won't be long now.'

Chase watched the kid run. Behind him now a few men looked out of the shops, the saloons along the way, perhaps guessing that something was in the air. It was another long ten minutes before the indistinct figure of a man appeared on the front porch of the adobe building, sent the kid scurrying away in the opposite direction and strode heavily toward a horse corral behind the office. He carried a Winchester rifle, obvious even at this distance.

'He sent the kid to round up his deputies,' Dan commented. 'Bigsby's not wasting any time.'

'I don't like the feel of this,' Chase said, speaking honestly.

'Nonsense!' Dan's eyes were filled with rebuke.

'Everything's going as planned.'

Dan Quick's eyes were sharply focused as he watched the events on the street of Van Horn unfold. First, a number of men appeared. Three or four could be seen racing toward the stable, one pausing to speak with Sheriff Bigsby. These, presumably, were the sworn deputies. Following them a trickle of men emerged from the saloons and other establishments. Bigsby chased one or two of them off. These would be men who offered to join the posse for excitement or had been egged into it. One of the men Bigsby sent away reeled as he walked and stumbled as he stepped on to the boardwalk in front of a saloon.

Sheriff Bigsby was already mounted on a buckskin horse when the first of his men rejoined him after retrieving their mounts from the stable. Other men swung aboard horses left up and down the street tied to hitching rails in front of various businesses.

All of these crowded around Bigsby, who spoke to them loudly enough that his voice was audible on the knoll where Quick and Chase Carver watched, although the words could not be distinguished.

'He's laying down the law to them,' Dan supposed.

It was only after ten more minutes when a few stragglers had arrived to join them that the sheriff led his band of men up the street and out of Van Horn.

'That's twenty men, easy,' Dan said. 'Russ Proctor

76

and his boys will have a time of it.'

It disturbed Chase slightly that Dan sounded pleased that the Kent bank robbers would have a time of it getting back to Bandolero, but Dan explained his thoughts: 'There go twenty armed men we won't have to concern ourselves with.'

He added, 'Let's give the town a little time to settle down. Then we'll make our move.'

Chase nodded. He stood as one bewildered, watching the normal morning traffic on the streets below. His mouth tasted sour; his eyes ached from the watching or from last night's whiskey, or both. He had already decided that he wasn't cut out for the outlaw life, but the energetic Dan Quick kept trying to bolster his spirits.

'This is it, my friend. In half an hour we'll be rich men!' he exulted.

Or dead men.

Quick must have read his thoughts in his eyes. 'Relax, Chase! The sheriff has cleared out and taken his deputies with him. You saw what he left behind – a bunch of barflies and slackers. We'll be in and out of that bank in no time, and that type aren't going to be riding our backtrail. Swing up on that horse of yours,' he finished.

Slowly they rode down the slope of the knoll, the still-low sun on their left. Dan explained the details of his plan as they rode. 'That alley,' he gestured, 'take it to the rear of the bank. There's a back door. It might be locked, but you can force it. I'm going to ride up to the front and walk in like any other customer. When you hear me shout, come in, and fast. They won't give us any trouble with guns in front and behind them. Just be sure to tie your horse securely. Without our ponies, we'll never make it out alive. And don't forget to reverse your bandanna and draw it up.'

Chase nodded and moved ahead like a man in a dream. Following the alley, he crossed to the rear of the green-painted bank building as he had been instructed.

He noticed that there were narrow iron bars on the two back windows, and the door looked stout. It was probably heavily locked, but perhaps not during regular business hours. Chase swung down from his pony and knotted its reins tightly around a hitch rail, remembering Dan's admonition. There was a warm breeze blowing from the south, rustling the leaves of a grove of mature cottonwood trees, which stood across the alley. A middle-sized white dog with a gray muzzle trotted down the alley and Chase watched it. Would he be badgered by these animals all his life? But the dog trotted past him and away again, only sneezing in passing as if he were somehow offended by Chase's presence.

No human being came into the alleyway. Chase pulled his scarf up over his mouth, drew his Colt, holding it next to his leg, and eased up to the door, placing his ear against the thick wood of it, waiting expectantly, fearfully, for Dan's cry which was the signal to break through it.

When it came it was startlingly loud as if Dan's

voice had been pitched higher by his own excitement. Chase put his shoulder to the door and
heaved. It didn't move an inch. He tried to imagine
what was going on inside by now, but couldn't. He
only knew that Dan was expecting him. Banging his
shoulder more roughly into the door he heard it
groan on its hinges, but it still did not open. He
thought about shooting the lock off but had never
tried such a thing, only heard of it, and realized the
bark of his .44 would likely bring men running and
defeat their purpose. He tried again, almost franti-
cally to break through, and felt the door give, heard
wood splinter in the doorframe. His shoulder was
already bruised painfully, but there was nothing for
it. He banged into the door once more and felt the
door give. Its opening was so unexpected that he
nearly fell through into the interior of the bank.

He crossed the interior of the offices quickly but
cautiously, and eased through another door in time
to see Dan, his face pale, his gun hand shaky, standing before two men – one a rail-thin, red-haired
man in shirt sleeves, the other an old, stout, balding
man in a town suit.

Dan glanced toward Chase and seemed to regain
his composure. 'I said I will have that safe opened,'
Dan said with quiet strength.

'Do it now!' Chase put in and the two captives
turned startled eyes toward him.

'My partner hasn't got the patience I have,' Dan
embellished. 'That's Mad Dog Carver and he takes
no prisoners.'

Chase was astonished to hear himself described in such a rough way, but Dan's words had the desired effect upon the bank manager and his teller. The older man ordered his assistant:

'Open it up, Tommy.'

'Yes, sir,' the teller said.

Chase waved his gun again at the bank manager and said, 'You can get busy emptying those cash drawers into a sack for us.'

In less than five minutes they were out of the Bank of Van Horn, Dan Quick easing out the front door after peering through the window at the, so far, silent streets, Chase carrying the loot into the alley behind the building. Dan had warned the two men in the bank about making any ruckus, and so far they had kept silent. Chase jammed the stolen money into his saddle-bags. He caught sight of Dan racing away up the knoll they had ridden down from. He was furiously flagging his horse's flank with his hat.

Chase grabbed for the tether to his blue roan and cursed. He had followed Dan's advice, all right, but he had tied the knot too tightly or the horse had drawn it tight, and for a panicked moment, he could not free the reins. With fumbling fingers he worked at the tight knot, fearing that at any second armed men would burst from concealment and find him trying to make his getaway with the town's money.

Finally the leather strips unknotted themselves and Chase shinnied up into the saddle, turning the little blue roan's head. The animal was swift, and Chase was never so glad as he was at that moment that it was. He raced up the flank of the knoll, in Dan's dust and never once glanced back toward Van Horn. No rifle spoke, no clamor was raised. In another few minutes he and Dan met up again on the far side of the knoll. They let their horses breathe while they sat their saddles, mopped their perspiring foreheads.

'That wasn't so much!' Dan laughed. 'A few minutes of excitement and a big pay-off. How much do you think we got?'

'I didn't have the time to even make a guess,' Chase said. Then he too started laughing. '*Mad Dog* Carver!' he exclaimed.

'It turned the trick, didn't it?'

'I suppose,' Chase reflected, 'but Dan – you gave them my name.'

'They won't remember that,' Dan said confidently. 'And they can't give a description of you. You were wearing a mask. Besides, by the time the sheriff gets back, we'll already be long gone.'

'Where are we riding?'

'Me, back to Bandolero, of course! I've got some unfinished business there.'

'I see.' Chase nodded. *Christine, of course.*

'Look, Chase, if you want we can stop right here and split the take.'

'I don't think that's a good idea,' Chase answered, glancing back toward the town. 'You never know – someone might be following.' He shook his head, 'I'll go along with you, if you don't mind. We can take care of that business later.'

They started on at a rapid but unhurried pace toward the land of the big mesa, riding back to the outlaw town of Bandolero, Chase carrying a mixed burden of triumph and fear.

SEVEN

The sky was clear with only a few scattered puffballs
of cloud as they neared the mesa road. Chase, who
had been teetering between terror and jubilance,
felt his spirits rise again as they made their way to
the shadow of the huge landform and started up
along the trail to the shelf where Bandolero sat,
huddled against the base of the mesa.

'What are you going to do first?' he asked Dan.

'What do you think?' Quick said with an easy
smile.

'Just ride up to the house and ask for Christine's
hand?'

'I can't think of a better time to do it, or any
easier way.'

'But the St Johns – Christine – will know that
you've been up to something illegal,' Chase said,
amazed by Dan's boldness.

'I suppose they will,' Dan said, tilting his hat back
a little with his thumb, 'but Christine will know that
I did it for her. St John – well he's seen a lot of

strange doings in his time. He might not like it, but the old bird must realize that he won't be around forever to take care of his daughters, that it's probably best for Christine to go now, while I have some money to take care of her.'

'I suppose so,' Chase answered dubiously. Dan's brashness had become a little reckless, he thought. Considering, he asked, 'What about Louise? Will you be taking her, too?'

Dan frowned, his forehead wrinkling. 'I guess I hadn't thought about that much – Lou and I don't get along well. If Christine says we should, I guess I'll have to take Louise with us, though it will complicate things.'

'Maybe Louise won't want to go,' Chase said. 'She might feel obliged to stay and take care of the old man.'

Dan's expression brightened again. 'You know, Mad Dog, you're probably right!'

Chase winced at the use of the hastily invented nickname. Quietly he asked Dan, 'Don't call me that again, all right?'

Dan laughed, apologized, said it was only a jest and guided his sorrel pony along the narrow trail, Chase riding silently beside him. Chase found his thoughts inexplicably concerned with Louise's future. He scolded himself mentally – what did he care about the dark-eyed girl? He had Laura Wheaton waiting for him back in the Colorado mountains, and he knew Louise St John not at all, really.

The sun was warm on their backs when they rode up through the familiar chute of gray stones where nopal cactus flourished. They rounded a bend in the trail . . . and found Jeb Tucker waiting for them.

He was squatted beside the trail where the rocks shaded him, holding the reins to his pony. He stood and dusted off his trousers as the two young men approached. He squinted at them and shook his head.

'I've been waiting for you two,' he said. 'We need to have a little talk.'

'What about, Tucker?' Chase asked curiously.

Tucker growled out his answer, 'I think I'd better talk to your partner here,' he said nodding in Dan's direction, 'You've already proved that you're slow to listen or learn, Chase.'

Dan swung down from his saddle, not reluctantly, for he had been sitting that piece of leather long enough. He had only kept going this long for Christine's sake. 'What have you got to tell me, Tucker?'

'What haven't I! Step back over into the shade with me.'

Chase swung down as well, holding tightly to the lead to his roan. He followed them to a natural bench of granite where Dan had seated himself next to Tucker.

'This sounds serious,' Dan said, tilting his hat back on his head again.

'Well it is,' Tucker agreed. He sat, legs splayed, gnarled hands clasped between them. 'You boys have played hell, you know?'

'I don't get you,' Dan said. Tucker gave him a look which indicated that he found Dan as thick-skulled as Chase.

'Well,' Tucker said with a thoughtful sigh as if he were looking for small words he might use when talking to a child. 'A couple of things. You did rob the Van Horn bank, didn't you?'

'Yes, we did,' Dan answered almost merrily. Tucker was far from merry.

'That's what I thought because of the timing. You realize that Sheriff Bigsby will be hot on the trail of Russ Proctor and his mob because of what happened over in Kent – you knew the boys were headed that way.'

'I realize that,' Dan said, 'that's why we—'

'Shut up and listen,' Tucker said in a tone Chase had never heard the old man use before. 'When Bigsby loses the trail from Kent, which he likely will since Proctor and Willie Lynch are good trailsmen and will have quite a lead on the sheriff, Will Bigsby will return to Van Horn and find that his bank has been held up as well. He'll be mad. He'll be more than mad, he'll be seething. The first thought that will come in to his mind is that it was a coordinated raid by the gangs of Bandolero.

'Then he will come, boys, and not with just a handful of deputies, but with all the men he can muster across Culberson County. There will be a public clamor to drive the Bandolero bunch out of here. They might even involve the army in it. Every man up here is in for a fight now.'

'I didn't think of that,' Dan said in a subdued murmur.

'That's not all you didn't think of,' Tucker said. 'In fact I wonder if you were thinking at all – what about the tribute you owe Kyle Jordan and Frank Butler now? You know they take a cut from everybody's poke after they've pulled a job.'

'But if I talk to them, they'll know that we started big trouble,' Dan objected.

'Yes, and if you don't, you'll have them good and mad. Everyone pays the price here.'

'But we—'

'And if you do tell them that you have money from Van Horn, the Boyer boys will know – they'd love an excuse to come after you again. *And* Proctor, Knight, and Willie Lynch will know that you used them and got them caught up in a big mess.'

'We can't do anything else but light out of this country, and quick!' Chase who had been listening silently said.

'And where will you go?' Tucker asked with a touch of nastiness. 'Sheriff Bigsby is going to want to find out who pulled off the Van Horn job, and any man up here will give your names up freely to save his own skin. If Kyle Jordan and Frank Butler have to leave Bandolero, after all the time they've invested in it, they'll put out the word for you two. They have a lot to lose – God knows how much money those two old pirates have stashed away, and if they're threatened with losing it, they will not

87

suffer it lightly, boys.'

Dan and Chase exchanged panicked looks. There was not a shadow of their earlier feeling of triumph on their faces. Chase asked quietly:

'What are *you* going to do, Tucker?'

'Me?' Tucker said with a meaningless smile as he stood to reach toward his horse's bridle. 'I'm going back to my small way of making a living. I've a few ideas how to make some money over in El Paso. It wouldn't be enough to interest big-time outlaws like you.' He swung into leather. 'I'm going back to my petty pilfering and small con jobs. It's not much, I know, but it suits me and keeps me comfortable.

'You boys,' he said as he turned his horse's head toward the desert below, 'seem as if you're about ready to swallow the dagger.'

Dan didn't catch Tucker's meaning, but Chase knew what he was talking about. They were up against it now, and likely had no way out.

Both young men watched as Tucker trailed off, saying nothing for long minutes. Finally, Dan spoke up. 'It's now or never, Chase – I'm going to get Christine. I'm getting her out of here. Are you coming with me, or do we split the money now?'

'I'd better come with you,' Chase said, placing a boot in the blue roan's stirrup and hauling himself aboard. After all, what was he to do on his own in Bandolero except wait and sweat? If Tucker had guessed what they had pulled off, others probably had. And it wouldn't be long before the Proctor gang returned to Bandolero, possibly with Bigsby's posse in full pursuit. Things were going to fall apart rapidly. 'If you want to get to Christine, we'd better do it now.'

Subdued now, they let their horses carry them up along the trail toward Bandolero. The town seemed strangely quiet, almost empty of people, though neither man had his concentration on it. They cut off the road leading through the outlaw town and rode directly toward the home of St John. The old Butler house looked ragged and weary, as if it were tired of its life on this lonely land. At least the chimney was still standing, Chase noted with some pride. If it made it though the first few days, the adobe mortar would dry in the sun and strengthen.

'Look there!' Dan hissed as they approached the house. Chase nodded, for he, too, had seen the gate in the white picket fence standing open. As he knew, St John never left the gate wide and seldom swung it in for anyone. Chase rested his hand on the butt of his holstered Colt.

'Something's wrong,' he agreed.

Dan had his rifle out, carrying it across the saddlebow. There was no movement near the house or behind the windows. No dog barked, no challenging voice called out to them. Yet there were no strange horses around, no sign of trouble, so maybe they were imagining things, with their nerves still taut from the day's events.

Chase began to swing down to tie his horse to the hitch rail, but Dan gestured and whispered. 'Let's tie up around the back. I have a bad feeling about this.'

His face was flushed, and Chase imagined that Dan's heart was racing as much as his, perhaps more so since his beloved was waiting for him. Was she all right? Had some drunken outlaws finally stormed the house when St John's vigilance had slackened? They rode slowly around the corner of the house. The back yard, too, was silent and empty. Chase wondered—

Where was Bobo?

If St John had fallen asleep or perhaps gotten ill, surely the big dog hadn't lost its own watchfulness. There was not so much as a bark, a whimper from the big dog inside the house. In the mottled shade of a scraggly, wind-buffeted cottonwood tree, Dan swung down from his sorrel pony and started toward the back of the house, his Winchester clenched tightly in his hand. Chase followed.

As they approached the back step, the door opened a crack and then was flung wide. Christine ran to meet Dan, to cling to him, sobbing.

'What is it?' he heard Dan ask in a voice he was trying to keep even but could not. It quavered as he held Christine at arm's length, studying her eyes, her trembling lip.

'Come in,' Christine said, her voice as unsteady as Dan's. 'I'll tell you there. But hurry and get inside – I'm afraid they'll come back.'

'Who?' Chase asked, but he got no answer as Christine hurried Dan into a long, low-ceilinged

kitchen. He heard Dan make a garbled little excla-
mation, which he might have meant to be a curse.
Following along, Chase found out what had caused
the muttered words. In a corner of the kitchen,
lying on a blanket was the unmoving body of Bobo.
His flanks and chest were streaked with blood. His
lip was curled back to show his fangs, but there was
no movement there. The dog was dead.

Christine's teeth chattered as she tried to speak.
'That's not the worst of it, Danny. Father's dead.
They killed him!'

'Who?' Dan exploded, gripping Christine's
shoulder tightly. 'What happened here? Who did
this? You have to tell me.'

'It was. . . .' she said, her voice faltering. 'The
men who were looking for you.'

'For us?' Chase blurted out. Christine shook her
head and looked at Dan again.

'For you, Danny! Those men were looking for
you.'

'The Boyer brothers,' Louise St John said from
an inner doorway where she stood holding her
father's double-twelve shotgun. 'I know who they
are.'

Her mouth was very tight, her eyes sparked. Dan
took one step in her direction.

'Your father is dead? What happened to you and
Christine?' he asked, not surprised to find that his
own voice was hoarse, shaky.

'Nothing happened to us,' Louise said, lifting her
chin high. 'Father wasn't the only one in this family

who knew how to use a shotgun. I put a load of buckshot into one of them, but they both got away alive.' She added this last bit as if she had failed at a simple task.

They went together into the parlor and sat on faded stuffed furniture around the cold fireplace. Little by little the story was told. The two Boyer brothers had ridden up to the house boldly. Someone had told them that Dan had been working around the house, and they meant to see him. Jeffrey St John had stormed out of the house with his shotgun ready, Bobo at his heels, and the Boyer boys had cut loose with their guns. Both had been killed.

Christine had screamed and run into the house, and the Boyer brothers, figuring that that must be where Dan was, rushed into the house after her. Louise had retrieved her father's shotgun and put a load of buckshot into one of them. Cursing and threatening revenge, one of the brothers had carried the other to his horse and made off toward Bandolero to find help for him.

'We'd better make up our minds now what we're going to do,' Chase said. glancing toward the open front door of the house.

'Christine is leaving with me, that's all there is to it,' Dan said, scooting nearer to Christine on the old sofa, taking her hand between his.

'How. . . ?' the woman looked baffled.

'That's what we always agreed upon,' Dan said a little sharply. He looked at her with disappointment.

92

'I know we did, Danny,' she answered, her eyes wide with confusion. 'But I never meant like this, this quickly.' She made a helpless gesture with her free hand.

'Neither did I,' Dan said, watching her eyes intently. 'But events have made up our minds for us. There's no staying here – not now.'

'I haven't packed. I haven't had the time to plan for this,' she objected.

'You don't need to pack.' Dan was insistent. 'Whatever you need I'll buy for you – new and finer things. I have the money now.'

Louise now glanced at Chase, asking the silent question – where had the money come from? He shifted his eyes away. He did manage to say:

'Someone had better make up his mind. The Boyer boys might have been run off but you can be sure someone will be back. Especially now. We had to have been seen riding past the town.'

'Yes, you're right, of course,' Dan said, getting to his feet. He struggled to tug Christine to hers.

'Louise?' Christine said, her eyes pleading with her sister. 'What should we do?'

'I guess you had better go,' Louise said heavily. 'The way things have turned out.' Her tone of voice indicated that she hated to give that piece of advice to her sister.

'What about you!' Christine asked, her panic returning. 'Surely you're coming too.'

Louise shook her head negatively. 'I can't. I've got to see to Father's burial. If anyone comes back, well, I've still got the shotgun.'

'You're not talking sense,' Chase said with some heat. 'If men start coming up here – and I think they will – you can't stay awake day and night protecting yourself with a single weapon. Later, how are you going to go to town to shop with no one to watch out for you? You know what the men in Bandolero are.'

'With your father dead, Kyle Jordan and Frank Butler may well want to reclaim this house for themselves,' Dan pointed out. 'They'd have every right to, you know. Whatever agreement they had with your father is at an end now.'

'You cannot stay here alone, Lou!' Christine agreed emphatically.

Louise hesitated. 'Father. . . .'

'Your father always took care of himself,' Dan said somewhat callously. It was obvious that he was eager to be going. His eyes continually flickered toward the front windows.

Louise's face was grim, her teeth clenched. She hurled her words at them. 'All right, then. Let's get out of here and let the place be damned!'

'Will we take the buggy?' Christine wanted to know, her own thoughts apparently now on practical matters. Her decision to go had been made for her. Obviously she needed her sister along for support.

'I think we have to, Dan said.

'I'll help you hitch it,' Chase volunteered. 'But, Dan – is there any other way out of here? By now we

94

might not have an easy run past the town and down the grade. They might even have posted sentries out to protect Russ Proctor and his gang from any pursuit.'

Dan paused and thought. 'There's the old Indian road,' he said. It used to lead all the way to the top of the mesa. There's an old abandoned cliff dwelling up there.'

'The buggy can't follow that road,' Louise objected. 'It's no more than a footpath.'

'She's right, I'm afraid,' Dan said with resignation. 'Well, then, there's only one way to do this and we'd better get to it.'

And hope the Boyer brothers hadn't gotten help and decided to come after them. And hope that the hills weren't crawling with sentries posted to keep any posse off the backs of Proctor, Knight and Willie Lynch as they returned from the bank hold-up at Kent. And hope that Kyle Jordan and Frank Butler hadn't somehow figured out that they were riding off without paying them tribute from the Van Horn robbery.

Other than that it should be clear sailing.

EIGHT

The air in the barn was stifling, heavy with the scent of rotting straw and manure. Old Jeff St John hadn't spent a lot of time cleaning it. Perhaps he had had no longer the strength for such chores. Dan backed the team of unmatched horses – including a black and a stubby little bay – to the traces. Chase tried to help, but he found his eyes fixed on the front yard of the house and the approaching trail beyond.

They began buckling the horses into the traces. 'Why do they want you, Dan? The Boyer boys, that is.'

Dan's fingers stopped their movement and his face seemed to freeze. 'It's all a mistake,' he replied.

'You owe them, you mean.'

'They think I do, but they won't listen to the truth of things,' he said almost irritably.

'How much?' Chase asked, pulling a buckle on the harness tight.

'It's not money,' Dan said, fixing a level gaze on Chase across the breadth of the two horses. 'They think I murdered their sixteen-year-old sister.'

'You didn't, of course,' Chase said.

'Of course not!' Dan snapped. 'I was working for them one summer on this little two-by-four ranch they have down in Jeff Davis County. The boys took off one Saturday to have a few drinks in town, leaving me alone with Rachel – that's how much they trusted me . . . then.

'Rachel loved to swim and it was a hot day, so I took her over to the river to take a dip. . . .' Dan's voice faltered, but his eyes remained steady on Chase's. 'She dove off the bank and hit her head on a rock in the river, and . . . broke her neck.'

Chase nodded his understanding. That must have been terrible – the end of her life on a bright sunny day. 'They blamed you,' he said.

'Of course! They called me a murderer. They were so angry they had to blame someone, Chase, and I was the man on the scene. They said Rachel had swum in that river all of her life and she knew where she could dive. I knew they meant to do me harm, and so at first chance I lit out for Bandolero – men had spoken of it before, and so I knew where it was. Well, Bob and Eric – those are their names – followed me and caught up with me here the night before you arrived with Tucker.' He smiled faintly and said, 'It was Bob's wrist that you broke when they had me cornered that night and decided to finish me off.'

Chase shook his head and tugged on the last bit of harness he had attached to the trace. It was a terrible story and he was almost sorry that he had asked. But at least he knew now why the Boyer brothers were so intent on getting their hands on Dan Quick.

'We're ready, I guess,' Chase said. 'I hope the women are. It's getting toward sundown already.'

'If we could, I'd wait until full dark to slip out of Bandolero, but we'd better get moving while there's still light on the trail,' Dan replied, taking the horses' bridles and leading them toward the barn door, the buggy rattling along behind.

The women were ready. At least, they waited, each holding a single carpetbag, in front of the house, Louise still wearing jeans and a long-sleeved shirt; Christine dressed in a light blue dress and straw bonnet. There was pain in their eyes, fear in the way they stood, watched and waited hopefully. Chase thought he had never felt so sorry for anyone in his life.

As Dan helped Christine up into the buggy, tossing her bag into the back, Chase told him, 'I'll get our ponies.'

Retrieving them, he led his little blue roan and Dan's sorrel around to the front yard as Louise, a black Stetson on her head now, held the reins to the team. She sat beside her sister looking miserable but defiant. Dan swung aboard his horse, glancing toward the west, either watching the declining sun as it lowered itself toward the mesa or the town itself, wondering where the Boyer brothers might be.

'Let's move out,' Chase muttered. 'I think it's

best we travel slowly through town. No sense in getting any more people interested in us.'

Cautiously they rolled down the road past the stubby yellow-grass fields that crowded the St John house. In Bandolero a few lamps were already lit behind the windows of the stone structures. The sun was fanning red light across the rim of the mesa and the sky was pink and deep purple in the west. The desert flats below were still bright with the light of day. The hub of an ungreased wheel squealed against the axle of the buggy.

There was activity in the saloons by the time they reached the road through Bandolero. A few men stood on the plankwalks in front. One of them Chase immediately recognized, the bear of a man with the silver-headed cane: Kyle Jordan. Beside him was a man with a face like a weasel. Hatless, his hair was ebony-black but it had a peculiar white streak running through it. He wore a suit and vest and a low-slung gun. His ferret eyes watched closely as did those of Kyle Jordan.

'Who's that beside Jordan?' Chase asked Dan as the two rode side by side, following the St John sisters in their buggy.

'Him? That's Frank Butler, Jordan's partner.'

The other patriarch of Bandolero. Chase would have no trouble recognizing him if their paths should ever happened to cross, which he prayed they would not.

Other men, some with beer mugs in their hands, stood watching in groups, their eyes fixed on the girls in the buggy. 'Keep moving,' Dan hissed to Louise who drove the buggy. 'But don't speed up.'

'Do you think they'll try to stop us?' Chase asked in a dry whisper as they rolled on, the squealing of the ungreased hub seeming unnaturally loud in the twilight hush.

'Jordan and Butler? They're likely happy to see the women leaving. They were stirring up too much trouble among the men. As for us – why should they care whether we come or go?'

'Unless word's reached them about the Van Horn bank job.'

'I don't see how it could have, but keep your gun close to hand and don't look around.'

Slowly they cleared the outskirts of Bandolero and reached the trail down through the rocky chute toward the desert below. No one was following them – Chase turned his head twice to make sure – but on the rocks which towered over the trail, he could make out four or five men with rifles above them. It was an unnerving sight, but Dan told him: 'They're on the lookout for Russ Proctor and his men, making sure that no one is following them from the job in Kent.'

'Do you think Sheriff Bigsby will be on their tail?'

'They'll have a pretty big lead on him,' Dan believed, 'and it's starting to get dark. No, he won't be able to find them – not today – but Jordan and Butler take no chances. That's how they've managed to hang on for so long in Bandolero.'

Dan sounded certain, but to Chase Carver every

shadow, each sound, held the possibility of menace. The wheel of the buggy continued to rasp and whine. Perhaps because of his age and infirmity Jeffrey St John had never gotten around to taking care of it. Perhaps, too, it was because the buggy was only used to go into Bandolero for supplies and it hardly seemed worth it to him to bother with. But the sound was growing annoying to Chase. He flinched when a low-flying owl flapped past them on its broad, flat wings and voiced disapproval.

Chase knew he was not a coward, but he also realized that he was not cut out for the outlaw life, never would be comfortable in it. He glanced at Dan who seemed unworried, nerveless, though he carried his Winchester across his saddlebow still. His eyes beneath the shadow of his hat brim were hawkish. Chase wondered what drove the man. He also found himself thinking back to Dan's tale of the death of Rachel Boyer. Was there something in that that Dan was not being honest about? The Boyer brothers certainly had not believed him.

Chase mentally shrugged his concerns aside as they emerged from the shadow of the mesa and rolled forward on to the desert flats where daylight, murky and vague, still illuminated its features. Dan now rode flanking the buggy, speaking to Christine, apparently trying to soothe her. Louise's face was grim as she drove the creaking buggy onward.

When they had put some distance between themselves and the Bandolero road, they pulled up to discuss matters. Dan swung down to assist Christine from the buggy seat. She clung to his arm, obviously trembling. Chase slipped from his saddle to join them. Louise seemed inattentive as she checked the harness and stroked the muzzles of her two horses, but Chase knew she was listening. Her entire future was related to their decisions as well.

'Well?' Chase asked, interrupting a bit of cooing between the two. 'What now, Dan?'

'We have to get farther away from the trail. Proctor and the boys will be along soon and there's a chance that Sheriff Bigsby will be on their trail. We can't take the risk.'

'What has the sheriff to do with us?' Christine asked, although she must have guessed by now.

'We just don't want to meet him. We can't go south, you know?' he said, speaking to Chase.

'No,' Chase agreed. That meant riding in the direction of the bank robbers and possibly the pursuing posse. The only towns in that direction were Kent and Van Horn which were not acceptable destinations.

'What's up north?' Dan asked.

'Mammoth Springs,' Chase said as much as he hated to even mention the town where he had dined among the dogs.

'How large is it?' asked Louise who had joined the group.

'Not large, but they do have a hotel there,' Chase said. He smiled at Louise in the dim light of dusk, but got no response from her for his attempted reassurance.

'How far is it?' Dan asked. 'Can we make it tonight?'

'It took me and Tucker almost two whole days,' Chase had to tell him. 'Of course, we weren't traveling fast.'

'Blast!' Dan said and then muttered a few more pungent words under his breath.

'This isn't much of a plan, is it?' Louise commented drily.

'It's the best we had,' Dan said with an edge of anger in his voice. 'All right – we'll strike out toward Mammoth Springs. We have to camp out tonight, of course.'

'We're going to sleep out here?' Christine asked. Fear had returned to her eyes as she studied the long, barren desert.

'I'm afraid so, dear,' Dan said, slipping his arm around her waist. 'After we've put a few more miles between us and Bandolero.'

'I wish I were home,' Christine said miserably. Louise turned her sister quite deliberately away from Dan and said:

'Well, we're not, and we can't ever be again. Let's just follow along and put our fate in the hands of these two. . . .' She couldn't find the word she was looking for, or subdued it. 'Men,' she finished.

Chase felt small at that moment. Although the whole proposition had been Dan's idea, still Chase felt guilty about dragging these two young women from their home, out into rough country where there were no conveniences of any sort, and little ahead of them that seemed promising.

'It's just like it was when Mother died,' Christine said gloomily. Dan heard her; as he helped her step into the buggy, he said:

'No, dear, it's not like that. Now you won't have to go live in an outlaw camp. There's a bright future ahead for the two of us, you'll see. I can take care of you very well now. Just be patient for a little while longer.'

Was Dan sincere, or just trying to calm the woman? Chase was starting to wonder if Dan Quick was just planning on using the woman for his own purposes or if he really loved Christine. The thought was unworthy of him, he decided, as he stepped into leather once again and the desert sky went to a deep purple slashed with orange to the west. He wished he had never asked Dan about the events that had put him on the wrong side of the Boyer boys. Now he could almost visualize the sixteen-year-old girl, smiling and waving, diving head first into the river, breaking her neck on some pleasant outing.

And at times other, more sinister images, presented themselves to him.

There were many ways a neck could be broken.

They traveled on until the shadows gathered, merged, and night finally spread a blanket of darkness across the cruel landscape.

'This has to be it for the day,' Chase announced. 'I'm bound to lose the trail. We can't go on, wandering aimlessly in the night.'

'You're right,' Dan said almost with relief. 'We can spread our blankets on that little knoll.'

'You mean we're going to sleep out here – on the open desert!' Christine asked in horror.

'That's all we have to offer,' Dan answered. There was a slight edge in his voice. Chase had noticed that he spoke that way with anyone who might be criticizing his choices. He tried soothing her again. 'It won't be bad, dear. And this won't last for long – I promise you.'

'We can take it, Christine,' Louise said. 'As the man says – it won't last long.'

She seemed to have some other meaning behind her words. Chase didn't waste his time pondering it. The buggy was drawn to the top of the sandy knoll and the women helped down. Chase spent a few minutes trying not to appear obvious as he scanned the area for rattlesnakes and other dangerous desert denizens.

Chase approached Dan as the women spread out their blankets and asked, 'Are we going to stand watch tonight?'

Dan looked toward Bandolero and nodded. 'I suppose we'd better. Do you want the first watch?'

Chase shrugged. 'It doesn't matter to me,' he replied. Dan nodded and walked away toward where the girls sat under their blankets side by side, knees drawn up, arms looped around them. Chase glanced at the Big Dipper, taking the time from the location of the natural clock's handle. Then he unsaddled his blue roan and let it nibble at the poor forage, taking his saddle for a perch against the ground. He sat down in the chill of evening, his saddle-blanket over his shoulders for warmth.

Nothing is as silent as the desert at night. No birds sound, no small animals can be heard scuttling around in the underbrush. Once, an hour into his shift as the others slept or pretended to, he heard the distant bark of a desert kit fox, but that was it. Chase kept his eyes on the southern horizon, though thinking about it he did not figure that any search party would have launched itself at that time of night. There was no sign of Sheriff Will Bigsby, of the Proctor crew, of the Boyer brothers – or Boyer brother, since Louise had shot-gunned one of them. No sign of Kyle Jordan nor Frank Butler. They were safe for the night.

Tomorrow might be a different story.

When he judged the hour to be somewhere after two in the morning, Chase walked to where Dan had made his bed and nudged his foot with his own boot. Dan sat up with a start and his hand dropped toward his holstered pistol.

'It's Chase,' he said quickly. 'Are you going to let me get some sleep?'

'Sure,' Dan said slowly. He rubbed at his head and asked: 'Nothing, no one stirring?'

'I'd have wakened you in a different way,' Chase told him. 'No, it's as still as a dead man's dance party.'

Dan smiled and reached for his boots. Shaking them out in case any scorpions, tarantulas, centipedes or such had crawled in to make themselves comfortable for the night, he dressed and stood. Almost to himself, Dan said, 'One more night out, that's all. Then we're home free, and with money in our pockets, Chase. You'll see – all of this will have been worth it.'

'I hope you're a prophet,' Chase muttered in return and went to make his own bed, twenty feet or so from the sleeping women.

It must have been an hour before dawn when Chase heard a scuttling sound near his bed. He gripped his Colt and opened his eyes to the starry darkness. He could scent her before she even reached his bed and so he lowered the hammer on the Colt and waited, wondering what she wanted.

Louise was on her knees beside him. Tentatively she stretched out a hand and touched his shoulder. Her kneeling figure was the darkest of silhouettes against the background of silver stars. He could not see her face, could only guess at her expression.

'I'm awake,' he said.

'Is there another way out of this?' she asked. It was cold enough that steam drifted from her lips, accompanying her whispered words.

Chase had been awakened from a dream in which he was returning to Timberline to meet Laura Wheaton, his pockets filled with gold. She had just emerged, smiling, from the house and was walking forward to meet him when Louise had approached his bed. Somewhat sourly, therefore, he asked:

107

'Do you mind telling me what you're talking about?'

'Keep it down,' she said in a whisper, glancing toward the edge of the camp where Dan was standing watch. She inched nearer to his bed on her knees. 'I don't like this,' she said.

'What don't you like?'

'Traveling nowhere with a man like Dan Quick.'

'Dan's all right,' Chase said.

'No he's not!' she replied, shaking her head emphatically. 'I don't trust him and I especially don't trust him with my sister.' Her voice lowered still further. 'He's killed before, you know.'

'Killed who?' Chase said, sitting up a little more. The moonless night was chilly.

'A woman – the Boyer brothers' sister,' she hissed.

'Who told you that?'

'The Boyers. This isn't the first time they've come to the house looking for Danny, though this is the first time things went so wrong. Once before – last summer – when Danny was cleaning out our well, they found out somehow and rode out to the house looking for him. Father and Christine were lunching at the table in the kitchen, so I slipped out to talk to them, to warn them what Father would do if he found them on his property. They said they didn't care, they wanted Danny Quick's hide and meant to have it.

'It just so happened that Danny had gone back to town to get something he needed for the job at the

108

well – a rope and a pail, I think – I told them hon-estly that he was not on the property. Then one of them – I think his name was Eric – proceeded to tell me what Danny had done: murdered their sister!'

'And you believed them?'

'Yes,' Louise said, 'I did. It was the way they said it, the anger on their faces.'

'I think they honestly believe it,' Chase said, now glancing toward where Dan would be watching the trail behind them, 'but that's not the way Dan tells the story.'

'Of course not!' Louise said as if arguing with a fool. 'You don't understand, Chase. I've seen the way he looks at Christine when he doesn't think anyone is watching. It's evil.'

'He looks at her because he loves her.'

'It's not like that,' Louise said, flipping a dismis-sive hand in his direction. 'It wasn't even like lust. I can't describe it, you would have to have seen it yourself. This is a bad man, Chase. I can't imagine why you are riding with him, but we have to get away – Christine and me. And so I ask you: is there a way out of this besides riding to Mammoth Springs? Something will happen along the trail. I'm sure of it!'

Her thin shoulders shivered. She wrapped her arms around herself. There was starlight in her eyes now, and Chase could read the deep concern there.

'I think your imagination has gotten the better of you,' he told her. 'Besides, I'll be along to take care of you. And, no I can't think of another way out of this, even if I were so inclined.'

'You're sticking with Danny. You're on his side.'

'Listen. Louise. I've never seen Dan Quick do anything to anyone. Do I believe his story? Yes. As far as breaking off from him, it can't be done. Not out here. Besides, he and I still have some unfinished business to take care of.' That was, they still had not divided the stolen money, something both men agreed was not the thing to do in front of the women. Let them have their suspicions, but they didn't need to see the evidence of the crime.

'I should have known I was wasting my time,' Louise said, scooting away. 'You're both the same, the same as every man who comes through Bandolero. One day I will run across a good man and I'll marry him the minute he asks, not caring if he's a dirt farmer, a clerk, or a layabout. So long as he's honest!'

With that, Louise crept away, and Chase rolled up in his thin blanket again, He knew he would not sleep any more on that night. There was already a hint of gray along the eastern horizon and it was the coldest time of the night. He lay, shivering a little, thinking the conversation over.

He wished he could recapture his dream, but now that he was awake it seemed only a dream. As for Dan Quick, it was true that Chase had believed him, but then Dan had had plenty of time to invent and practice a tale. Were the Boyer brothers right? Louise had offered no evidence beyond her obvious dislike of Dan and his affection for her sister.

Chase lay in the dark, wondering, not for the first time, if he should have just trailed away with old Jeb Tucker.

NINE

The desert crossing was long, heated, and dry. They had nothing to eat but some biscuits Louise had stuffed into her carpetbag with foresight. She had also brought a packet of coffee, but they dared start no fire, the smoke of which would have been visible for miles, out on open land as they were.

It was not that day but the next, after one more cold night on the desert, that they trailed into Mammoth Springs. Christine looked haggard and utterly weary. She sat slumped on the buggy's spring seat, hands clasped between her knees, her glazed eyes staring straight ahead as if they were unseeing. Louise seemed fresh, but her face was grim, set. They pulled up on the outskirts of town and looked it over. The morning streets were active, but not busily so.

'Is that the hotel?' Dan asked, pointing at the two-story white structure that could hardly have been anything else.

'That's it,' Chase answered.

'You see, Christine,' Dan told her. 'We've made it. I promised you it wouldn't be long. Now you can have a bath and a good meal. Later you can go out and buy yourselves some clothes and whatever else you need. This will be the start of our new life together.'

Dan sat his sorrel horse close to Christine. She only glanced up and gave a weary nod; there was no smile of relief. With disgust, Dan yanked his horse's head aside and rode up beside Chase again.

'Well? What are we waiting for?'

'I don't know if I should go down there with you,' Chased answered slowly. Dan looked perplexed. 'There's a small matter of my horse and this saddle,' Chase told him. 'Tucker got them for me, and I doubt they've forgotten.'

'Got them from a stable?' Chase nodded. 'Well, aren't there other stables in town? There must be.'

'I guess so.'

Dan smiled and slapped Chase's shoulder. 'Well, go find a place to board your horse. What's the matter here – am I the only one who's happy to be off the desert with saddle-bags filled with money? Chase, if it bothers you that much, go along later and ask the man if he needs payment for the horse. You can afford it, you know.'

'I guess that's what I'll do,' Chase agreed. It had hardly seemed like a crime at the time, and he was in desperate need, but he could understand the stable owner holding a grudge about a missing horse and saddle.

'Fine! Let's get going then, folks. We have a lot of living to do.'

With Dan leading the way and Chase following along after the buggy, they trailed down into Mammoth Springs, reaching the main street via an alley that sketched itself between the familiar stable and a boot shop. Chase left it to Dan to see to the stabling of the horses and the care of the buggy – hopefully he would remind the man to grease the wheel hubs. Chase hung back in the shaded alley feeling a little uneasy. The blue roan could smell the other horses, water and fodder in the stable, and kept urging Chase to follow along, but he was not yet ready to face the man in there. First he would eat, buy some fresh clothes, and shave.

Sitting his pony in the alley, a few people passed, glancing at him incuriously. One man with a red shirt and leather vest and an outsized nose stopped and looked long at him. He had a wondering look in his eyes and so Chase asked him: 'Can you tell me where I can find another stable?'

'Don't like this one?' was the response.

'I had some bad luck with them once.'

'You can go up this way two blocks,' the stranger gestured, 'and off to the east another half block. There's a man named Mendoza who can help you.'

'Thanks. I guess I'll give him a try,' Chase said. He turned his horse immediately and started away, feeling that the man's eyes were still on him. Of course, that was probably a false notion. A guilty feeling can bring all sorts of imaginary concerns with it.

Chase was now riding parallel to the main street along another, broader alley where he passed a feed barn and an open blacksmith's shed. Mendoza, when he found him, was a small, round, nut-brown man with a friendly smile. Chase swung down heavily, glad to be out of leather again. The blue roan was led away to join a handful of other ponies in a wide pen. Chase noticed something was being built on the property, probably a barn so that Mendoza could successfully compete with the other stable which had an enclosed shelter for horses – a necessary convenience in winter weather.

'Your horse,' Mendoza said before Chase, saddle-bags over his shoulder, left, 'it is a fine animal. Have I not seen it before?'

Chase sifted through a few lies he had prepared for such an occasion, and finally just answered, 'I don't think so,' and strolled away.

Entering the hotel lobby, he again felt an uneasy twinge of guilt. He glanced at the desk, but did not recognize the man behind it, nor was Chase recognized. Dan was sitting tilted back in one of the plush chairs in the lobby, his hat dangling from his fingers. Chase crossed to where he sat.

'How's it going?' Chase asked.

'Fine. Sit down, Chase!'

'You got the girls a room?'

'I did. The finest room in the hotel. Both of them

looked tired and sulky, but after a few nights in a good bed and a couple of good meals, they'll perk up again.'

'I hope you're right,' Chase said.

'Of course I am. Give a woman comfort and she's content.' Chase had placed the saddle-bags between them on the floor.

'You'll be needing some money,' Chase said.

'Not just yet. Leave it where it is for now. I'm still living off the money old man St John paid me for my work on his well and the chimney. We're fixed for a little while.'

'I guess I have enough for a room, too,' Chase said, thinking. He plucked at the front of his faded blue shirt and told Dan. 'And, I have got to get myself a new shirt. Seems I've had this one on for ever.' In fact, he nearly had – since Timberline, anyway. He had slept out in it, eaten with dogs, labored on the chimney, and ridden many miles. He had to smell of sweat, horse, and dog.

'Find a room,' Dan advised, 'and have them bring a tub and start filling it for you – that's what I did. I'm just waiting until they've filled it. Then we can both go out and buy some fresh duds. You'll feel like a new man.'

Dan had checked into the hotel earlier. Now Chase got the key to a room. He trudged up the stairs and found the place easily. Opening the door he looked around, walked to the closet, and stashed the saddle-bags there. The door was still open when a young man, one Chase had not seen before, knocked, poked his head in, and asked:

'Will you be wanting your bath sent up now, sir?'

'Please,' Chase said. He kicked off his boots and stretched out on his back on the bed. He was yet a little in wonder at the idea of a hotel where they brought your bath to you.

He was still uneasy about being in Mammoth Springs. He had no idea how Tucker had covered their tracks or if the old man had even bothered. It didn't matter, he supposed, he had enough money to clear up any debts someone might feel he was owed. He was probably worried about nothing. After a while two boys returned with a zinc tub, which they set up near the window. One of them glanced curiously at Chase, and he wondered if this was one of the boys Tucker had tricked on his last visit to the hotel. Chase reminded himself mentally to make sure the boys each got some silver money after they had filled the tub.

Later, after soaping and scrubbing himself down and sitting in the tub until the water went cold, he rose, shaved, and peered at himself in the mirror. Not a different man, but a better one. He hated to put his old clothes on again over his fresh bath. No matter what Dan had planned; he sent one of the boys off to at least buy him a fresh shirt. Other articles could be seen to later.

Standing shirtless at the window as the tub was emptied and hauled away, he saw a stagecoach rumble into town, greeted by screaming boys and yapping dogs. The few idlers he could see along the boardwalk didn't bother to rise, barely glanced that way. It was so much easier to be a kid. And a lot more fun.

Dan arrived as Chase was buttoning up his new white shirt.

'Couldn't wait, huh?' Dan said with a smile.

'My old shirt was just about stiff, Dan. I couldn't stand the thought of wearing it again.'

'I know,' Dan said, sitting on Chase's bed. 'But from now on we won't ever have to go through any of this again – old clothes, worn-out ponies, down-at-heel boots are all things of the past.'

'You think we got away with it then?' Chase asked, turning from the mirror to face him.

'Partner, I know we did!' Dan said without a doubt.

Chase wasn't so sure. They had made one county sheriff very mad. And by now, Kyle Jordan and Frank Butler must have figured out what had happened. Then there was always the Boyer boys to be considered – even if one of them had been shot up pretty badly. Besides, Chase had no liking for Mammoth Springs. Maybe Tucker had greased their way out of the town, but Chase was still riding what could be a stolen horse and sitting a stolen saddle.

'When do we split the money?' Chase asked as they exited the hotel into the bright sunlight.

'What's your hurry? Planning on running off on me?'

'I don't like this place and I've got another place I want to be.'

Timberline. *Laura Wheaton*. Was she still waiting for him? Of course she was. She was a faithful girl, but Chase had ridden off without much to promise her. Still, a girl can get tired of waiting. She couldn't imagine him coming back rich, as he was now. Then an odd thing happened as he and Dan strolled side by side down the boardwalk. Chase found that he could no longer draw an image of Laura Wheaton's face from his memory. That was impossible, wasn't it? She was the reason behind all of this, his motivation. Otherwise he would never have started down the outlaw trail.

They passed a bulletin board outside the stage station where a man in rolled-up sleeves was tacking up a new wanted poster which must have come in on the stage.

'Look at that,' Dan said, nudging Chase. They halted. When the man stepped away from the poster, Chase could read it clearly.

Wanted for robbing the Bank of Van Horn
'Mad Dog' Carver and unidentified accomplice.
Contact Sheriff Will Bigsby, Van Horn, Texas.
Reward offered for capture of Carver . . .

There was more, including a description, which was accurate if vague since Chase had been wearing a mask at the time. He felt his heart tighten up a little.

'I told you that you should never have used my name,' Chase said angrily. 'Even the greenest

119

robber knows better than that.'

'Calm down,' Dan said as they walked away. 'If that's the best they can come up with as a description – six feet tall, dark hair, blue eyes – what are you worried about? There's hundreds of men around that look like that.'

'You didn't read it all, apparently. It also said that I was riding a blue roan. There aren't hundreds of them running around.'

'So,' Dan said, indifferent to Chase's problems, 'get rid of the horse. You can afford a new one.' They had come to the mercantile and Dan was admiring a striped suit in the window. 'Are you coming in?' he asked.

'I'll take care of that later. Right now, I've got to do something about that blue roan.' What exactly, he did not know. Maybe the best idea was to do what its last owner had done, simply abandon it. Still, anyone looking for that horse and for 'Mad Dog' Carver could find it easily at Mendoza's place.

Thinking along those lines he walked on down the street. He was just passing a milliner's shop when he saw Louise and Christine exiting the store. Christine was now wearing a red dress which looked to be made of velvet, though Chase knew little about these things, and wore a small red hat with a black feather in it. She had a pleased look on her face. Louise did not look so happy. She was still dressed in jeans and a white shirt, and was carrying a few boxes from various women's shops, She halted as she saw Chase, taking Christine by her elbow to halt her.

'It looks like you've had a good morning,' Chase said.

'Yes, we have,' Christine said, smiling prettily.

'You look a little better yourself with a shave and a new shirt,' Lou said.

'Thanks.' He pretended to admire Christine's dress. 'It was nice of Dan to give you some money for outfitting yourself. It wasn't wasted.' Both women stared at him, Christine a little coolly.

'Danny didn't pay for this,' Louise said. 'You see—'

Christine interrupted her sister. 'I want to get all these things back to the hotel and sort them out,' she said. Louise shrugged and handed her the boxes she had been carrying. With a light step, and a smile over her shoulder at Chase, Christine started toward the hotel.

'Where were you headed?' Louise asked.

'Nowhere in particular. How about some breakfast? Or have you eaten?'

'Not yet. Where would we go? The hotel's the only place to eat I know in this town.'

Chase knew of another but you had to eat at the back door. He replied, 'Me too, and their food's probably as good as any other we're likely to find.'

Together they started along toward the hotel; Christine could be seen, just going in through the white door. 'I think there's an entrance to the restaurant on the side,' Chase said. For reasons he did not go into with her, he wished to avoid the hotel lobby as much as possible. One of Tucker's victims might see him and remember his face. He had enough trouble without going through something like that.

They found the door they were looking for, were seated at a table, and tried to decide if it was breakfast time still. The little restaurant was neat, cozy, pleasant enough. The matronly waitress who came to seat them recommended the fried chicken, which they could smell cooking. They both agreed it would be a good idea.

Waiting, Chase asked his questions in a low voice. 'You are sure Dan didn't give you any money to buy those clothes? He promised that he would.' And why was Dan so reluctant to tap the money in the saddle-bags? They still hadn't discussed divvying it up.

'No, it wasn't his money,' Lou said, tilting her head back so that the lantern light caught her face prettily. 'What can you expect of a man? They'll promise you anything.' Her voice was not bitter, but only disappointed in the entire sex. Being a part of same, Chase felt obligated to say:

'I'm sure he meant it about taking care of Christine.'

'Are you?' she asked. Feeling protective of her sister? Probably, and Chase had forgotten how much Lou disliked Dan for whatever reason.

'I know he's got a little money tucked away,' Chase remarked and Lou's lips tightened a fraction.

'I think he's probably got a *lot* tucked away,' she

said. 'What I'd like to know is where it came from.'

That backed Chase into a corner, and he had nothing to say as the waitress returned with a platter of crisp fried chicken, a great bowl of mashed potatoes, and four ears of sweetcorn on the cob. They began eating in silent enjoyment. Chase watched Lou's eyes as she relished the meal. He had almost forgotten that the woman hadn't had a decent meal in nearly as long as he had, and he felt vaguely guilty that he had not remembered that.

After filling his belly so well that there was only a single ear of corn and a dab of potatoes left on the table, he asked another question that had been bothering him.

'Where did it come from, then? The money for the new clothes?'

'Is that your business?' Louise asked a little sharply.

'No, you're right. It isn't any of my business, I was just working around the question of why Dan hadn't given you girls some of that promised money.'

'I'm sorry,' Louise said, seeming to mean it. Her long dark hair gleamed in the light of the lantern on the wall; her black eyes seemed to have softened. Maybe the food had brought her a sense of well-being, taken the edge from her anger. She continued.

'Father had money saved. You see . . .' she said, dropping her voice to a confidential tone. She hesitated and then said, 'Well, I guess it doesn't matter anymore if I tell you. It's all tied up in the reason

Kyle Jordan and Frank Butler agreed to let Father have the old Duncan house, why we went to Bandolero in the first place.' She paused as the waitress took their empty plates away, declined any dessert, and waited as the woman walked away. 'It was no accident that we went there after the trouble down in Valentina. Father never talked about it, but one hears things, you know. From what I was able to piece together, my father had something that could implicate Jordan and Butler in the murder of a marshal.'

'Is that why the two old bandits set up out there in the first place?'

'It may have been,' Louise answered. 'As I say, I only got hints and bits of information when one of the two would come out to talk to Father. They promised that he could have the house as long as he lived – and they paid him fifty dollars every month just to stay there.'

'Hush money?'

'If that's what they call it. So you see, we were prisoners there in a number of ways. Jordan and Butler would not have let Father just ride away, knowing what he did. Of course, they knew he had troubles of his own and was unlikely to go.'

'But you. . . .'

'Christine and I were no threat to them – if we did know anything it would never stand up in court, being only hearsay. And frankly, we don't know anything.' She shrugged. 'They are probably happy to be rid of us.'

Chase digested this as he let his meal settle. Fishing his last few dollars from his pocket – money from working on St John's chimney – he paid the check. He realized that he was now nearly back where he had begun – stranded in Mammoth Springs and broke. He decided that he was going to tap into the bank money whether Dan was ready to split it or not. Ten dollars, twenty dollars is a lot of money when your pockets run dry. He would take that much, no more and even scrawl an IOU to be stuffed in the saddle-bags. Surely Dan couldn't object to that. Chase needed some pants; the seat of his jeans was wearing thin.

'I'm going to go up to see how Christine is coming along,' Louise said as they rose from the table. Suppressing a yawn, she told him, 'I might even take a nap.'

Chase could understand the impulse. He wouldn't have minded some sleep himself, but there were several things to be taken care of. First, the blue roan. He decided that he would offer to sell it to Mendoza, who had seemed to like the pony. He would make up some story – he had found another horse he wanted to buy, but was short on cash. That would do. He would let Mendoza bargain him down, and in the end take anything the man offered. He hadn't come up with a plan for selling the tooled saddle – the one that Tucker had bought, or stolen, for him. How was old Tucker doing? he wondered. Probably better than he was.

As Louise entered the hotel lobby from the

restaurant, Chase went out into the sun-bright street via the side door. There was no way to get to Mendoza's without going past the jail and town marshal's office, but he steeled himself for that. No one had cause to stop him and question him. There was that vague poster out for 'Mad Dog' Carver, but it was so short on detail as to be almost useless.

He strode confidently down the plankwalk, passing a hardware store, the millinery shop, a shoulder-wide bar, each with its own species of patrons. On the next block, he stepped up on to the plankwalk again and saw a vaguely familiar face. A bulky man with a very prominent nose, wearing a red shirt and leather vest stood in front of the jail, smoking a thin cigar, speaking to a man who looked to be a farmer. There was a badge on the big man's vest now. Chase felt his heart rise in his chest. He had met the man before . . . in the alley next to the stable. This was the man he had asked for help in finding a place to hide his blue roan; the town marshal, who must by now have read the Wanted poster out of Van Horn.

Cursing through gritted teeth, Chase veered away and started walking across the dusty street as a hay wagon and two riders who might have been cattlemen in their town suits passed. No voice called out for him to halt, and he quickly merged with the shadows of the alley flanking the stable.

It was there that the men jumped him.

TEN

There were three men waiting there for him. Chase recognized only one of them. One of the Boyer brothers. His brother was not there – the one that Louise had shot – but he had brought help with him. The first man to grab Chase got hold of his shirt and spun him to the ground. He hovered over Chase as he rolled over. He had a thick, curly beard and tiny eyes. The second man was nearly as big as this one, but he wore only a mustache and was red-headed. Boyer waved his arms gleefully as if he were about to go crazy.

The two big men took Chase under the arms and slammed his back against the stable wall, driving the wind out of him. To help it on its way, the bearded man drove his fist into Chase's stomach. That blow seemed to trigger Boyer off. He stepped near enough so that Chase could smell him, see the sweat on his face, the rage in his eyes. His contribution to the fun was to slug Chase in the jaw, once on each side. Grinning, Boyer stepped away while the big men kept Chase pinned to the wall.

'Where is he?' Boyer demanded through clenched teeth, his eyes glittering. This one had to be Eric Boyer unless he was a quick healer, since Dan had told him that it was Bob's wrist that he had broken with his pistol barrel. That also meant that Bob was running in poor luck, since he had to also be the one that Louise had shot.

'Where's who?' Chase tried. A big hand shot out and clenched his throat, driving his head back.

'Oh, he's a funny one, Eric,' the bearded man said, tightening his grip. Boyer replied:

'Don't break anything, Sal. I still want him able to talk once he gets the idea that we're serious.' Sal's grip slackened slightly. Chase tried again.

'He's gone,' he said in a voice reduced to a whisper.

'What do you mean?' Boyer demanded. 'Let his throat go, Sal.'

'Dan Quick rode on. To a place called Pocono.'

'I know where it is,' the redhead said. So did Chase – he had passed the town on his way down from the mountains. There was a trading post there and six or seven small houses, nothing more.

'What did he go there for?' Boyer wanted to know. 'And why aren't you riding with him?'

'He said he wants to set up there,' Chase answered. 'He says no one comes around much and he wants to buy a few acres and maybe build a house.'

'And he left you behind!'

'It was sort of a mutual agreement,' Chase told the furious Boyer. 'We've been doing a lot of riding, and I wanted to try out some town life for a change. And the girls wanted to rest and buy some clothes and such. I said I'd stay with them until they were ready to travel on.'

'What girls?' Boyer asked angrily. Sal told him.

'Those St John girls, Eric. Remember, I told you I saw them riding out with Dan and his buddy here.'

'Yeah, I remember now,' Eric admitted. 'What in hell are those two doing with you?'

'They had to get out of Bandolero. With their father dead. . . .'

The red-headed man was smiling, revealing broken yellow teeth. 'That's a good story as far as it goes,' he put in. 'But if it's true, how is it that that sorrel pony Dan Quick rides is in this stable?'

'He traded off,' Chase explained. 'He thought he'd be harder to recognize on a different horse, and besides that sorrel is pretty beat-down.'

'Mister,' Eric Boyer said threateningly, 'you'd better be telling the truth or we will come back and pound your head to mush.'

'What is the trouble between you?' Chase asked. 'Does he owe you money?' He watched Eric Boyer's eyes flash again. Boyer answered deliberately.

'He owes us my sister's life,' he said. 'And unless he can figure out a way to give that back, my brother and me will track him down if it takes the rest of our lives.'

'Your sister?' Chase said as if he had not heard

the tale before.

'Yeah.' Boyer hesitated, took a slow deep breath and said, 'I'll tell you just so you know what kind of rat you're hooked up with. Me and Bob sold a few horses and we decided to spend some of the money in town, drinking. We left Rachel home on the ranch. We sure couldn't take her to no saloon. Dan Quick had a little cabin on the property – he was working for us off and on. We swung by there first and warned him to stay away from the house, and he swore he would.

'Well, he didn't. As soon as we were out of sight he went over and talked Rachel into going for a swim. It was dreadful hot and Rachel was fond of swimming anyway. When we came back. . . .' The tough man's voice broke. When he had regained his composure, he went on, speaking carefully now.

'Dan was waiting when we got home. He said he had some bad news for us. He told me and Bob that Rachel had dived into the river, hit her head on a rock and broken her neck. She was laid out on her bed. Bob and me rushed into the house and found her dead. Dan took that time to climb into his horse's saddle and get off the ranch.'

'But if it was an accident. . . .'

'It wasn't an accident,' Eric Boyer roared loudly enough that two men passing the mouth of the alley paused to look their way. His voice lowered, still holding menace. 'It wasn't an accident. A neighbor lady had come over, offering to help clean Rachel up for a funeral if we wanted. She pointed out the bruises on Rachel's arms. They were finger bruises; there's nothing else that looks like them. And at the back of Rachel's skull, the woman found where a clump of her yellow hair had been torn out.

'No sir, she had been beaten and then her neck broken. I don't know if he ever told you any different, but if he did, he was lying. That man took our sister out to the river to do her wrong. I'll tell you something about Dan Quick – the man just is not normal. Sixteen years old,' he said as if to himself. The volume of his voice again increased.

'You'd better be telling the truth about Pocono,' he warned Chase, 'because if he's not there, we'll be coming back to look for you again. And by now you've learned one thing about me and my brother: we don't give up.'

He nodded to the bearded man. 'Say goodbye to the man, Sal.'

Sal swung a meaty fist against the side of Chase's face, and his knees buckled before he fell to the ground. He could hear their boots thumping against the alley as they tramped away, but he could not lift his head to watch them. It felt as if his own neck had been broken by Sal's savage blow.

He must have passed out for a while, for he had been in sunlight when he entered the alley but now he found himself in shadow.

He levered himself to his feet, using the facing wall for support. Staggering to the mouth of the alley he saw nothing, no one special. People were moving around town on their usual errands, living out unremarkable lives. He blinked into the sunlight, stooped to pick up his battered hat, and started on his stumbling way toward the hotel.

He had to find Dan and warn him to get out of town. He was having serious doubts about Dan's version of Rachel's death now, but he didn't intend to see the man hung either. It would make Christine's odyssey in vain, and Louise's sympathetic love for her sister would darken her spirits as well.

He realized that he could not stand to see Louise hurt.

There were still tiny lights spinning behind his eyes as he entered the hotel lobby. He crossed it this time without caring what anyone thought of his appearance and made his way to his room. It was like climbing a mountain just getting up the stairs. Entering, he caught a glimpse of himself in the mirror.

His face was rubbed dark with alley dirt. There was a lump on each temple where he had been struck, and a larger one on his jaw where Sal had told him goodbye. This was already changing into bruised colors. There was a trickle of blood from his right ear.

His new shirt was torn out at the elbow and it was filthy. His jeans were no cleaner than they had been. Angrily, Chase sailed his hat toward the bed. He rinsed off his face and let his blurry eyes stare at the blurry eyes in the mirror.

Going to the closet, Chase found that the saddlebags were still where he had left them. With fumbling fingers he undid one of the straps. Crouching in the closet, he removed two bank-fresh five-dollar notes he would need to pay for new clothing from their band. He crumpled the bills, and stuffed one into each pocket. not wishing to be noticed passing uncirculated notes. Crossing the room again, he sat at the small desk and opened a drawer. There was paper inside and envelopes, along with a few pencils. Deliberately he wrote across the head of the paper 'IOU' and underneath in smaller letters printed 'I needed ten dollars.' Then on a whim he inscribed it with the name 'Mad Dog Carver'. It did not make him feel any better, but somehow it brought a smile to his lips. He tore this bit of paper from the sheet and folded it.

As he returned to the closet, he paused before crouching again to insert the note in the banded five-dollar notes. He glanced at it again and won-dered – was Dan Quick just trying to be funny when he gave that name to the men in the bank, or had he done it deliberately so that Chase's name was the only one attached to the wanted posters, so that Chase and not Dan was the bank robber, the outlaw? His head ached too much to long consider that question. Placing the note inside, he buckled the bags shut again and stood with the intention of going out for some new clothes. He only made it halfway across the room before his head began to reel and the floor to circle. He barely managed to stagger to the bed where he let gravity flop him on to the mattress. His eyes were open, but the world was going dark again. With no defense against it, he gave up and let the night which should have been day fall again.

He slept deeply but unpleasantly, still aware of trouble. An hour or so must have passed, judging by the changing shadows in the room. He could not remember where he was. He thought he must be out on the desert once again, for the same figure approached his bed and asked the same question as before:

'Is there another way out of this?'

One of Chase's eyes opened and a sort of reality returned to his battered brain. Louise St John sat beside his bed in one of the stiff wooden chairs that furnished the room.

'Hello,' he said numbly.

'Forget hello – what happened to you?'

'Eric Boyer happened,' he muttered, sitting up in bed as well as he could.

'He's here?' she asked with shock.

'Well, he was,' Chase answered. 'This is his work. I don't make a practice of beating myself up.'

'What did he want?' Louise asked. She leaned forward, intently studying his face.

'Dan,' Chase said. It was painful to move his jaw.

'What did you tell Boyer?' she asked.

'I lied. Told him Dan had ridden out toward Pocono.'

'I see. Why didn't you just give Boyer what he wanted?'

'Dan's life?' Chase shook his head. 'I couldn't do

that.' Louise sighed and sat back in her chair, folding her hands together between her knees. She poked at her hair, studied his face, and asked:

'What are you going to do now, Chase?'

'Find Dan and blow town before Boyer gets back.'

'And where are you going?' she asked.

'I don't know,' he had to admit. 'Anywhere, since anywhere has got to be better than before I met up with Dan, with Jeb Tucker.'

'Was it that bad?' she asked with some concern. Chase recalled the cold, the hunger, far too vividly. He would never live that way again.

'It was bad.'

'You're going to continue to ride with Danny Quick?'

'No, not with him. We've still got a matter to see to, that's all.' Splitting the bank money, of course. After that he wanted nothing more to do with Dan Quick, nothing more to do with the outlaw way. He had always had it in mind to return to Timberline, to Laura Wheaton, of course, but now the idea seemed shopworn. How that could be, he did not understand. Louise leaned forward in her chair again, her eyes damp, genuinely concerned.

'What was it you used to do for a living, Chase?'

'Ranch-hand,' he said, rubbing his jaw, which was still sore. At least the man, Sal, had not broken it.

'That's honest work. Why can't you try it again? Surely someone would take you on.'

Why? Because he was now a man on the run, a

bank robber, 'Mad Dog' Carver, with a price on his head. He would be watching over his shoulder for the rest of his life. Louise waited for an answer. Getting none she asked another question.

'Do you think Danny is planning on taking Christine along with him?'

'I don't know. I thought that was his idea all along. Why do you ask?'

'I don't think she will go now. It's not like being rescued from Bandolero now, is it? She likes this town, and I think I do, too. I suppose it's not much, but it's more than we're used to. It suits both of us. We'd never make big-city women, anyway. Mammoth Springs has everything we want or need. Christine's already made a friend. Even that's a new experience for her. We've never had friends in all our lives.'

'You're thinking of staying around here?' Chase asked in surprise. Well, he considered, why not? Louise was right; to women who had been held as if in prison, Mammoth Springs must seem to be a fine place indeed.

Louise's eyes were steady on Chase's own. 'Christine's friend is a man named Hugh Bonner. He's a land developer in a small way. He's built six cottages to the east of town. Two bedrooms each on small lots. He is only asking fifteen hundred dollars apiece for them. Christine and I could afford one.' Chase's face must have reflected his surprise. The women were serious about remaining in Mammoth Springs, it seemed.

'I've seen the homes,' Louise said. 'Ours would have a large elm tree in the front yard.' She sounded as if they had already made up their minds, selected one of the cottages.

'How can you afford it?'

'I told you once, Chase – Father was given fifty dollars a month by Kyle Jordan and Frank Butler for having kept silent about something he knew. We never spent much; we grew most of our own food, wore the same dresses for years. Father wasn't cheap; he was frightened of what might become of us after he was gone. We lived in Bandolero for ten years – since we were only children. Fifty dollars a month for twelve months of the year times ten . . . even with what we did spend on necessities, it added up over time.'

'Your father was right in doing what he did, though it must have been hard on you,' Chase said.

'We never felt deprived.' She shrugged. 'Anyway, since neither Christine nor I drank whiskey, what would we have spent money on in Bandolero?'

Chase laughed. It pained his side where he had taken a few blows to the ribs. Louise rose.

'Are you sure you have to ride out with Danny Quick?' she asked, standing over him.

'I do,' Chase had to tell her without explaining why.

'Well,' she replied with a muffled sigh, 'if you ever get back this way, I'm pretty sure we'll still be here. Look us up. You know, Chase, there's one thing about hard-living men – they don't usually last very long.'

He said nothing and Louise turned toward the hotel room door. Pausing as she reached it, she told him: 'If you plan to go looking for Danny Quick, he should be easy to find. He's parading around town in a new striped suit.'

Chase watched the door after she had slipped out and closed it, trying to arrange his thoughts. These had clouded and altered into new shapes. Still, he had to at least go out and find some new clothes to wear. Eric Boyer would not be gone forever, and when he did return he would be breathing fire.

He walked down the street at this hour before sundown. Looking around for Dan as he made his way toward the dry goods store. Feeling better about himself, he emerged from the store wearing a stiff new pair of black jeans and a dull red shirt, and went looking in earnest for his partner.

Dan wasn't hard to spot, even in the crowded saloon where Chase found him. He was standing at the bar wearing a smoke-gray suit with narrow white stripes – the same one Chase had seen him admiring earlier.

Chase slid up to the bar at Dan's elbow. Quick glanced at him with a broad smile. 'See you got some new clothes ... and a new face. What happened?'

'Eric Boyer was here – guess who he's looking for.'

'You don't mean it!' Dan said, the color draining out of his face.

'I do. I sent him off on a wild goose chase, but he'll be back. We have to light out, Dan. Now.'

'All right,' Dan said, placing his unfinished glass of whiskey down on the bar. 'Have you got the goods?'

'Still at the hotel. Let's catch up our horses first, then we can swing by and pick than up.'

'Right.' Dan tried for a smile, but it was a sickly expression. 'Let's not waste time.'

Dan started for the stable while Chase strode toward Mendoza's place. He had decided to ride the blue roan after all. It was better to get it out of town. The marshal had already read the Wanted poster with its description, and he had been eyeing Chase too closely. It was better to get the pony out of there than leave it to jog the marshal's memory should he come across it.

Chase paid Mendoza and watched anxiously as his horse was saddled. The animal was frisky, ready to run after its rest, and it felt good to swing into a familiar saddle on to the known pony's back.

They arrived almost simultaneously at the hotel. Dan walked toward Chase and looked up at him. His face was still pale, his mouth tight with tension. 'Get the bags. I'll see to the bill. Then we're shut of this place.'

Chase nodded. He swung down, having noted that Dan had not said a word about the girls. Whatever his intentions had been before, he now obviously wanted nothing to do with anything or anyone who would slow down his escape. Chase returned with the saddle-bags filled with stolen money to find Dan mounted again. He fastened the bags behind his saddle and swung aboard. Then they were riding out of Mammoth Springs and out on the desert, heading nowhere as fast as their horses could carry them.

On the run again.

ELEVEN

Chase had to push the little blue roan to keep up with Quick. Although the little cutting horse was quicker than Dan's big sorrel, it hadn't the stamina of the larger animal. And Dan was riding hard, meaning to make his run long. Already the sun was fading, the shadows before horses and men long, sketched weirdly against the rugged rock and sand of the desert. Chase didn't bother to ask where they were heading. Dan likely had no answer for him. They were just racing hard away from any pursuit. And there would be pursuit, both men knew that. Eric Boyer was not the sort of man to give up. He had already proven that.

With the sky reddening, Dan finally drew his shuddering horse up on a low cactus-stippled rise and let it blow. The roan, quick as it was, as fresh as it was, did not like the treatment it was receiving and let Chase know it with a tossing of its head, the stamping of a front foot.

Chase said, 'No one's going to catch us in the

night. Let's find the best spot we can and camp.'

The eyes that Dan turned on Chase were glittering strangely. His lips were drawn back to show his teeth. He looked more animal-like than human.

'I'm riding all night,' he told Chase, and as he said that he slicked his Colt revolver from his holster. 'I suppose you can stay here – after you let me have those saddle-bags.'

Chase saw it all, suddenly. He had been a fool. The reason Dan had avoided splitting up the money became obvious: he had never planned to share it in the first place. It was easier to keep it all together for the time being.

'You dirty dog,' Chase said with a shadow of sadness in his voice. 'To think I trusted you.'

'We all make mistakes,' Dan sneered. Then, as Chase ducked reflexively behind the blue roan's neck, Dan fired his revolver.

Chase felt the horse shudder and bunch itself instinctively for a run, but the bullet had killed it instantly and it began to roll to the ground. Chase kicked out of the stirrups and leaped free as Dan's pistol spoke twice more. The first bullet slapped into the dead horse's body, the second, fired as Chase rolled away, ticked off Chase's ear, digging a shallow groove in his scalp in passing. Dan had barely missed his killing shot.

Chase was on his knees, partly concealed by the blue roan's body. His revolver was already in his hand. Dan's silhouette was vivid against the crimson sky; Chase shot him three times. Dan reeled in the saddle, half-twisted around, and then fell to the rough ground. Chase did not rise quickly. He had no doubt that Dan was dead – there was no hurry. Besides, his legs felt weak. His hands had begun to tremble. He was not sure at first that he could rise.

Gradually he lifted himself from the ground and stood beside the still-heated body of the blue roan in the settling gloom of the desert night. Then he made his way to where Dan lay and made sure the man was dead.

Chase was weary, his mind filled with thoughts both angry and remorseful. Of one thing he was certain: he could not spend the night in the vicinity; he had never been fond of ghosts. Removing the saddle-bags from the roan took a deal of effort, but when he finally had them free, he walked to the sorrel, which stood placidly, seemingly not spooked by the game the humans had been playing.

Tying the saddle-bags on behind Dan's saddle, he swung aboard and walked the sorrel out of there, into the blackness of the wasteland night.

It was shortly after dawn two days later that Chase Carver trailed into the still-sleeping town of Van Horn. His nerves were ragged, his body sore, his stomach empty. He wondered as he entered the town limits what he had been thinking when he made the decision to return here. But he had made up his mind and there was nothing to do now but see it through.

He found a small restaurant not far from the

sheriff's office. Through the front window he could watch it across the street as he ate a stack of hot cakes and drank three cups of dark coffee, dawdling. The waitress was starting to eye him suspiciously, or simply impatiently, when the door to the sheriff's office swung open and a tall man stepped out on to the plankwalk, smoothing his hair before placing his hat on.

Chase had never seen Sheriff Will Bigsby close enough to identify him, but this man was wearing a silver badge that glinted in the new sunlight of morning. Chase rose and paid for his meal, and went out into the crisp new day himself, still reluctant, still determined. He left the trail-weary, deprived sorrel where it stood as he slipped the saddle-bags from behind his saddle and crossed the street, watching the back of the man he assumed to be the sheriff as he slowly strode about, making his morning rounds.

Chase walked to the office door, knocked twice, and swung it open. Behind the sheriff's desk sat a sleepy-eyed, narrow man with a cup of coffee raised halfway to his lips.

'Sheriff Bigsby here?' Chase asked.

'You just missed him,' the thin man answered, nodding toward the door.

'A man said to give him these,' Chase said, and he placed the saddle-bags on the desk. Then he turned and walked out, crossing the street quickly, half expecting a voice to cry out and call him back, but none did. He walked the sorrel out of town and made his way on to the desert once again.

Chase found himself smiling suddenly. He had neglected to remove the IOU signed by 'Mad Dog' Carver that he had placed in the saddle-bags with the bank's money. Ten dollars – had a bank ever been robbed for that little gain? Still, it had been a serious crime, but somehow, although Sheriff Bigsby might be keeping his eyes open, he doubted they would mount a man hunt to track him down. Not now.

But *now* what was he to do? He couldn't return to Timberline, to Laura Wheaton, that seemed certain. Likely he would be shot on sight. Louise had asked him why he couldn't look around and find some sort of ranch work locally. Well, why couldn't he? A law-abiding life seemed a noble pursuit after all that he had been through.

The first thing to do was check on the girls. Louise had told him that they had a plan and the money to carry it through, but that might have been just hopeful thinking or a few words to ease Chase's concern. He did not know how much money they had. Nor did he know this man, Hugh Bonner, that Christine had taken up with. He owed it to them to check up on things. And, to be honest, he owed it to himself to see Louise at least once more.

The traveling was slow. He took pains to spare the sorrel. There was a fair amount of water to be found here and there, but little in the way of graze for the animal. The big horse was exhausted by the time he reached Mammoth Springs again.

At the hotel he was informed that the women had checked out days before. 'I believe they bought one of those little cottages Hugh Bonner built out along Arapaho Road.'

'Where is that?' Chase asked.

'Not more than half a mile out of town, due east. Odd place to live if you ask me, but the folks out there seem happy enough with what they've got.'

Chase thanked the hotel clerk and walked the sorrel over to Mendoza's stable. The new barn was already rising, most of the framing done. The Mexican spotted him, raised a hand, and sauntered over from the building site.

'Hello!' He looked at the worn-out sorrel and shook his head. 'You used him plenty hard, huh?'

'There wasn't any choice,' Chase said.

'I know – these things happen. I will take good care of him.' Mendoza took the reins and asked, 'What happened to that nice little blue roan you were riding?'

'Oh that—' It was a borrowed horse. I gave it back to the man who owned it.'

'I see.' Mendoza looked as if he wanted to ask another question, but did not. Chase wondered if the town marshal had gotten to thinking about the blue roan on Mad Dog's Wanted poster and come around looking for such an animal. At any rate, it seemed like a good idea to distance himself from the horse.

'Do you have another horse I could use for the day?' Chase asked. 'No hard riding – I'm just going out to Arapaho Road.'

'A couple,' Mendoza said. 'I'll show them to you; you can take your pick.'

Mounted on a stubby little serviceable bay horse, Chase rode out half an hour later, the bright rising sun in his eyes. Arapaho Road was easy to find. It had been newly graded and had a freshly painted sign attached to a post. Hugh Bonner's way of attracting potential buyers, he guessed.

Riding that way he saw a cluster of small-frame buildings facing each other along the street which went no farther than the end of the development. Bonner was doing all right selling the cottages, it seemed. Chase saw a few kids playing in one of the back yards, an old woman sitting on a porch knitting. He could see why the hotel clerk didn't think much of the houses as a place to live. He was a town man, used to the benefits of that. A man used to living on a ranch wouldn't have cared for the nearness of his neighbors. But he could see why such a place would suit Louise and Christine. Neighbors to talk to; near to town so that they could drive in and purchase whatever they might need. It was a far cry from Bandolero's roughness and the isolation of the home they had there.

Chase halted the bay horse and looked along the street. Six cottages. Well, Louise had told him that theirs would have an elm tree in front, and there were only two that did. And the first was the house where the old woman sat knitting. He started the horse toward the one on the opposite side of the road. That must be it. It had a very small barn beside it, painted with the same fresh white paint. The breeze shifted the shade beneath the elm. Was this the house? Chase felt oddly reluctant to find out, to see Louise again. She had found her little niche in this world and he had arrived bearing no gifts but his trail-dusty, ragged, beat-up self.

He swung down from the bay and stood on the edge of the property, looking at the cottage, still hesitating. There was a white post with an iron ring mounted on it and he tied the bay horse's reins to it. He was still undecided, still uncertain as to whether this was even the home of the St John sisters as he started up the path toward the porch.

He was halfway to it when the front door opened a crack and the dog burst forth. Dog? No, a pup with fuzzy, pure black fur. It looked to weigh about five pounds and have five pounds of hair. It rushed to Chase, its rear end wriggling, wetting the ground under it. As it reached him it rolled on to its back showing its pink belly.

Chase glanced toward the porch and saw Louise in a blue print house dress, a white apron over it. He grinned at her.

'Bobo?' he asked, rubbing the slightly damp belly of the pup.

'But twice as mean,' Louise said with a smile. Chase picked up the puppy and carried it to the porch where he put it down. The pup continued to sniff at him and twice to grab hold of his pant leg and roll around in exquisite happiness.

'He does bite,' Chase said, removing the pup's fine teeth from his trousers.

'He's still young.'

'Is he always this eager?'

'I'm afraid so.'

'You don't suppose he'll turn out like Bobo, do you? This is going to be a big dog, you know.'

Louise squatted to pet the dog, which writhed with pleasure at her touch.

'Bobo was trained to be the way he was. By Father, to watch out for us. This is just a little pup, and if raised right he will remain so even when he's full grown and quite ferocious-looking.'

'You seem to have a lot of confidence that it's so,' Chase said.

Louise straightened up and looking directly at Chase said, 'I am always confident, even when I'm wrong.' Chase stood pondering that statement as the puppy continued its mad antics before settling down to scratch its ear. 'Come in and have a look around,' Louise invited.

'All right. Thanks. I've been wondering about the place. Is Christine at home?'

'No, she's out riding with Hugh Bonner. I think they're planning on getting married in a few weeks.'

'Isn't that kind of fast?' Chase asked as they walked through a small living room, sparsely furnished with a leather sofa and matching chair.

'It is, and it worried me for a while. The only man she's ever known before was Danny Quick. I hate to see her rush into anything, but Hugh is an honest, level-headed, hard-working man. The first time he saw her he was obviously smitten. I think Christine has her mind made up, and truthfully, I don't think she's made a mistake.'

'All you can do is wish her the best,' Chase said as they walked down a short hallway with two facing bedrooms and returned to pass through the house to the small kitchen.

'The windows are well set up to catch the evening breeze, and it cools off the room when the oven's been going. I know it must seem a tiny place to you. . . .'

'So long as it suits you. Like Christine's man, Hugh, if he suits her, who am I to offer comments?'

Bending down to look through the small kitchen window he could see that the back yard at least was large. There was room for chickens, goats, and a garden – whatever Louise had in mind, for she surely had thought of these things.

'How about water?' he asked.

'One deep well for all six cottages,' Louise said. 'We all get our money back if it ever goes dry.'

'You have that in writing?' Chase asked, having heard such promises before.

'Of course,' Louise said. 'Father didn't have much to give us, but he constantly lectured us on the vagaries of the law, especially when it came to property.'

'Well, then, I think you have done yourself proud.'

They returned to the living room followed by the

pup, which had now settled down from the excitement of meeting a new human friend and lay watching them, head on its front paws.

Louise said with some heaviness, 'Well, I tried my best, but now you know, Christine it seems, will never even have the time to settle in here. Hugh Bonner has a large house on the other end of town. I'll be sitting here, a lonely spinster, in a few years.'

'You can find someone for a roommate,' Chase said. 'A shop girl or a waitress from town, maybe.'

'That's too far for them to walk to work every day,' Louise sighed. 'And to stumble home at night on that rough road. But you're right – everything does work out somehow. Have you found a situation yet, Chase?'

'I just got back, woman. Have I had the time to even look!'

Louise laughed as Chase had meant her to. It was a hearty if low-voiced laugh and the sound of it was cheering. Thinking back, Chase could not remember ever hearing her laugh before, but then her life had not been one filled with abundant laughter.

Louise made them a nice little meal of ham sandwiches and hard-boiled eggs. After eating and thanking her for her effort, Chase decided that he might as well ride into town, return Mendoza's bay horse and recover the sorrel. On the porch, Louise, sanding very close to him, looked up and said, 'You will be careful, won't you?'

'Very careful from now on,' he promised, and surprising him, Louise went to tiptoes and kissed him lightly on the lips. He pondered the meaning of the kiss all the way to town.

He found Mendoza in a state of excitement, talking to two of his stable boys. Dismounting, Chase led the bay toward him.

Puzzled by the sense of excitement, Chase asked, 'Is something going on around here?'

'Not now,' Mendoza said. 'I see you took care of the bay as you promised.'

'I told you I was just taking a short ride.'

'You would be surprised what people do around here,' Mendoza said, taking the lead to the bay. 'This morning – aye! – it was terrible.'

'What happened?' Chase asked as they walked toward one of the pens. He saw the sorrel, looking fine and fit.

'Three men came here and tried to steal some horses,' Mendoza told him with a frown. 'I did not like their look and sent one of my boys off fast for the marshal. It was a good thing I did, because these three, they just started taking my horses. Their old mounts were sweating and shuddering – they had ridden them very hard from somewhere.'

'Did you know them?'

'No. They were not from around here. The marshal, he told me later that one of them was a wanted man named Eric Boyer. They had probably ridden up from Bandolero. That, the marshal said, was because the army had raided the place; it's a known outlaw hideout.'

As he spoke, Mendoza undid the cinches on the

bay's saddle and slipped its bit, turning it into the pen.

'Did the marshal arrest them?' Chase wanted to know.

'No, sir. Boyer, he decided to swallow the dagger – do you know the expression?'

'I've heard it a time or two.'

'The three of them started shooting, although the marshal had brought five men along with him. It didn't last long. Two deputies were wounded, all three of the outlaws died.'

Chase shook his head, many thoughts going through his mind. Finally he said, 'I never thought that life around a stable could be so exciting.'

'Ah,' Mendoza said with a humble gesture, 'it is all part of the job. Shall I get your sorrel for you?'

'Yes. I won't be riding him far or hard any time soon either. Not now.'

TWELVE

Louise had started a vegetable garden in the back yard and so Chase volunteered to help her till the soil. The ground was hard; it had never been turned. The black puppy, eagerly joining in, had probably turned as much earth as Chase had before Louise called a break in the afternoon. The sun was high, hot, and she had made lemonade.

They drank it in the shade of the front porch, the pup at Louise's feet.

'In a few months,' she said happily, 'the hot weather will end and the seeds will already be sprouting.'

Her enthusiasm was like a child's. A lot of that must have to do with the way she was forced to grow up. Had she ever truly had a childhood? Chase had told her what he had learned from Mendoza about the fate of Eric Boyer, and the news that the army, no doubt goaded on by Sheriff Bigsby, had raided that nest of outlaws – Bandolero. Louise had little to say; she didn't seem to want to revisit the past.

154

'It's about time,' was her only comment.

Chase considered – if not for the bank robbery in Van Horn, would Sheriff Bigsby ever have gotten stirred up enough to summon the army? He never had before, apparently content enough to let things go on as they were, with outlying towns like Kent bearing the brunt of the depredations. Another reason the patriarchs of Bandolero, Kyle Jordan and Frank Butler, would have been furious if they had discovered Dan Quick's plan to hit the county seat, Van Horn, itself.

Chase, like Louise, had no wish to revisit the past. His life as an outlaw had been one long painful experience, nothing more. He should have listened to Jeb Tucker long ago if he wanted to live outside the law and become a competent petty grifter where the stakes were low, but the penalties much smaller.

That, too, was not for Chase. He had stumbled into the life of a thief, and he doubted he would like being one at Tucker's level either. He saw where it led – ask Eric Boyer; ask Dan Quick. Chase was content for the time being just being alive, sitting on the front porch of Louise's cottage with her near, sipping lemonade on a sunny afternoon.

The fuzzy pup at Louise's feet twitched and rose, its head canted, listening, and in a moment they saw the buggy approaching the cottage. Christine St John was dressed in a white dress with yellow trim and a tiny yellow hat. She was smiling widely as the buggy drew up, driven by a young, handsome, but shy-appearing man with fair hair who had to be

Hugh Bonner.

Christine slid from the seat, nearly tangling her feet in her long dress. She rushed toward Louise and hugged her, crying and laughing at once.

'We're married,' Christine said, barely glancing at Chase.

'But you can't be!' Louise was obviously stunned.

'Do you need to see the license?'

'I mean – you always wanted a fancy wedding. You didn't even invite me!'

'We were passing the courthouse,' Christine said, 'and we decided on an impulse. Hugh ... Hugh and I were growing very impatient.'

'What are you going to do? Where are you going?' Louise asked. 'Come in and tell me all about it!'

The two swept into the house, leaving Chase alone on the porch. It seemed the thing to do, and so he crossed the dry yard to walk to where Bonner waited on the buggy. Chase stuck out his hand.

'Congratulations.'

'Thank you,' Bonner said, seeming flustered.

'It was kind of sudden.'

'Yes, wasn't it? I think I've still got the shakes.'

'It'll all work out. Once it's an everyday thing, I'm sure she'll be a comfort to you,' Chase said.

'Your name's Chase, isn't it?' Bonner said, struggling to make conversation. He kept glancing toward the house, waiting for Christine's return.

'That's right. Friend of the family.'

'I know – Christine's mentioned your name.

What is it you do for a living, Chase?'

'Ranch-hand, mostly. I haven't had a chance to look around yet.'

'Maybe I can help you there,' the young man said earnestly. 'I have a friend – Kyle Stuyvestant – he owns the Running S Ranch not far from here. He was asking about help in finding some men for his next roundup.'

'I'd be obliged if you could put in a word for me,' Chase said.

'Why sure, nothing easier.' Bonner's eyes had returned to the cottage again. 'Christine said that she just needed to pick up a few things,' he told Chase. 'What does that mean to a woman?'

'I wouldn't know.'

'Tomoriow we'll be back to pick up all of her stuff. I guess they told you that I have a new house on the other side of town.'

'I heard. You seem to be doing well, Bonner.'

A glow of pride flushed the man's cheeks. 'I am making my way pretty well,' he said.

'Good for you.'

The conversation flagged again. Bonner was obviously eager to start on his way. Chase could not blame the man.

Bonner tried to rekindle the talk they were having. 'We've certainly had a lot of excitement around Mammoth Springs lately.'

'Mendoza was telling me about it,' Chase said.

'How did he know?' Bonner looked baffled.

'It happened at his stable,' Chase answered. 'The

horse thieves were shot down there.'

'Is that so!' Hugh Bonner reacted with surprise. 'I suppose I'll hear about it eventually. What I meant was the death of the killer, Mad Dog MacCray – whatever his name was.'

'I guess I didn't hear about that,' Chase said carefully.

'Yesterday it was. The marshal found his body out on the Van Horn trail. He'd been dead for a few days, but there wasn't much doubt as to his identity. He was riding the same blue roan as on the poster. The horse was dead beside this Mad Dog. It was still wearing that fancy-tooled saddle. The bank robber had been shot three times, probably by his unidentified accomplice. That ends his life of crime.'

'He swallowed the dagger.'

'What?' Bonner's face went blank.

'Nothing, just an expression I heard today.'

'Oh, I see. The only thing was, there was no positive way to identify the man, but the marshal seemed to have no doubts – you know how the law likes to clear these cases as soon as possible. But some folks were still wondering if it was really Mad Dog who died.'

'I'm sure it was,' Chase Carver answered. 'He'll never be back.'

There was a rising ruckus from the house, and Christine and Louise, giggling, hugging, and whispering stepped out on to the porch again. Regaining her ladylike composure, Christine started back to the buggy, carrying a few boxes filled with her necessaries. Bonner jumped down to help her store them in the buggy and help her up into it.

Chase watched as Bonner started the team homeward, toward Christine's new life. Then he turned and walked back toward the young woman in the blue dress who stood watching from the porch, the black fuzzy pup bounding and stumbling clumsily at his heels.